The Decades

The Decades

six stories | six authors

The AdNibs Collective

451
Editions

The Decades
© The AdNibs Collective, 2025
Authors: Seán Coffey, Máirín Stronge, Sharon Guard, Gio, Sarah Lou Ryan, Conor Clohessy

First published by 451 Editions, 2025
Electronic Edition by 451 Editions, 2025
www.451Editions.com

ISBN 978-1-9162975-3-1

All rights reserved
The moral right of the authors has been asserted

This book is sold subject to the condition that it shall not, by way of trade or otherwise, be lent, resold, hired out, digitally reproduced or otherwise circulated without the publisher's prior consent in any form of binding, cover or digital format other than that in which it is published and without a similar condition being imposed on the subsequent purchaser. No part of this book may be reproduced in any manner without written permission, except in the case of brief quotations for review purposes.

Cover concept: Sarah Lou Ryan

Book design and production by www.Cyberscribe.eu

Icons used for illustrative purposes in the book are sourced from www.AdobeStock.com

Printed in Ireland by www.SprintBooks.ie

The Decades

Contents

1: DANNY, 1964   9
2: SHAUN, 1978   31
3: NINA, 1989   56
4: ELIZABETH, 1999   83
5: THE CASEYS, 2007   102
6: ANONYMOUS, 2018   133

    The Writers   162
    Acknowledgements   164

1: 1964

DANNY

As far as I can see there's always grit in life. Bitty, grainy, hard stuff bigger than dust and smaller than stone. Not soft like beach sand that's been rolled smooth by the ocean. Angular and abrasive. Useful, by times – emery paper, the wet-and dry, the golden sheets in my uncle John's carpentry workshop, every grade. Grit for traction, working a heavy-goods from Newcomen Junction up to Connolly on a frosty December morning. Or facing out of Kent Station for Dublin Hill and the Rathpeacon Bank on a wet October evening with the Heuston service, the rails slick with fallen leaves. Working the lever in the cab, scattering it every which way.

But CIE gave up on it – the practice of gritting the rails, because it's not always good, the grit. Wearing metals, destroying bearings. Grit in your barrel, grit in your shoe. My poor dear Nancy, God rest her, lips together, tongue moving, tasting her custard, her disappointed expression – 'ah, it's a bit gritty' she'd say. The smarting eye on a blowy summer's day, the irritant. That's grit too. The little thing that spoils everything. The sight suddenly gone from an eye, a tear even. That how the news about Larry got me.

It was spring '74. I'd been certified for passenger service on the Sligo line weeks earlier, but I hadn't been rostered, I was too junior. Still left mucking around North Wall on coal and mixed-goods. But this particular Friday evening in April it finally fell into my lap and boy was I proud. The 15:10 service from Connolly to Sligo MacDiarmada, Driver Daniel M. Freyne. Two Class 121s coupled hood-to-hood, one hundred and twenty-eight tons of American muscle hauling a set of seven Inchicore-built Cravens, sixty-four passengers in each, plus buffet car plus brake car, full to capacity that Friday evening.

I notched her up passing Croke Park feeling ten feet tall, me the youngest mainline driver in the company, and I have to admit on the final run in from Collooney my heart was full. I was riding the very rails the poor old da had tended as a humble permanent-way man for forty-six years. And as luck would have it, I'd seen in the circular that there'd be a team out at Bridge 53, and sure enough as I rounded the curve at restriction speed there was his old buddy McGloin to give the signal. Did I not give him some blast in return, opened the window, let a roar at him, the lads copped-on, waved, punched the air. Local boy makes good.

A clear run into MacDiarmada, green at Distant, green at Home, eased her to a halt on Platform 1 exactly at the sign, just so. All Trains to Stop Here. Sam Collingwood the station-master and a few of the boys out to congratulate me and reminisce about the da, how proud he'd be. He was dead three years by this time.

And that was that. I got her formed up for the return, had a cup of tea and a sandwich, and was standing out the back enjoying a smoke in the evening sun when Feeney the ticket-man sidled up to me. A sleeveen, I never liked him.

'Did y'hear the latest,' he said. 'Yer old buddy Larry MacGowan went to cut the throat but he made a hash of it. So he's in the Mental now. Place for him, that he may never lave it. He's a nuisance to himself and everyone else. Always was.'

Maybe it was the mood I was in, but the news fair turned my head. Ten years gone, ten years in Dublin, ten years forging ahead, I'd never once looked back. Never needed to, never wanted to. But now I did, now I had to. Poor Larry in the Mental Hospital, of all the places. Guilt, was it, I felt then? – I only know that it caused me to blink, grit in the eye, a tear wiped away. Larry in the Mental. Of all places.

The Mental: there and not there, looming over the town or invisible, part of the daily run or completely ignored and unknown. High walls to keep them in, the lunatics, high Victorian chimneys for the fires to keep them warm, a farm to feed them, churches Catholic and Protestant, and a graveyard to bury them in. Full of people from the County Leitrim, so the da said, there was no one in it from Sligo. 'He's gone into St Columba's,' was enough to say, more than eloquence, more than a story, it was the end of reputation, any social standing whatsoever. There would be no way back for Larry after this.

Thanks to Auntie Maura ours was a house where the Mental did have presence. She was a kitchen attendant there, and her stories fed our imaginations every bit as well as the leftovers she brought fed our stomachs, kept our kitchen above the average for a permanent-way man's family. She was unmarried, a gambler, owned a Morris Minor that she drove to the races in, and was mildly disreputable. The ma was the elder, and never were two sisters less alike, the ma being Church-stricken and very dogged and fixed with it.

'Wait until I tell yiz,' Maura would begin and our ears

would prick up. Ward Nurse John Connolly trying to get Packy McGrath to take his medicine:

'I'll take no medicine from you, John Connolly.'

'C'mon Packy, be a good lad.'

'John Connolly, go away from me with that bottle.'

'You'll take your medicine Packy McGrath.'

'I won't, I won't, John Connolly.'

'McGrath, you'll do it in the end.'

'I won't, John Connolly. Didn't I ride your sister Breda up agin d'wall, I did, John Connolly. I rode your sister Breda up agin d'wall.'

At this Maura would burst out laughing, the da would smile, the ma would bless herself and tell her she was a disgrace and to think of the child. That was me. But she'd finish her story. 'It took three of the lads to haul Connolly off him, and McGrath laughing all the while. Oh he's very mad, that Packy McGrath, but cute as they come.'

Another time.

'Wait until I tell yiz. Do you know who's in now?'

'No.'

'That latchiko Paddy Henry. He heard the Guards were coming for him and he signed himself in. Isn't he after getting the two daughters pregnant, the youngest is only fourteen. Isn't he some yoke?'

'Mother of God,' the ma blesses herself, a guffaw out of Maura.

'Well, if you saw what the lads do to his dinners. I won't even say. Except the dinners visits the toilets before they gets to Henry, if he but knew it. Oh they do love to watch him eating them.' Another cackle. That was Maura. That was the Mental. Full of people mad or bad or both. But Larry was neither. It just wasn't right.

Maybe every quiet, shy child needs to have a friend like Larry. I certainly did. A doer, a risker, a messer, someone who coaxes them to take that extra step down the road of life that can make all the difference. That they'd never take on their own. I was an only child where Larry was the sole boy amid a big gaggle of sisters in a house as noisy and rambunctious as ours was sedate and respectable. We lived close by each other and sort of grew together over the years, falling into our roles so that though younger than me, and smaller, he behaved more like an older brother, at times mocking, as times encouraging, at times wise beyond his years, or so it seemed to me. But be it football or fishing or just fooling around, he was always fun, that was the thing.

I remember. It was the Tuesday of the last Easter holidays of our national schooling. 1964. I know it was a Tuesday, because Tuesday was the day that those Mental patients who could be trusted were let go downtown. And Larry's da had him detailed to cycle into Sligo and win him some cheap plug. Because they got a stipend, each of them, in cigarettes or pipe tobacco, and for those souls who didn't smoke what good was it to them. Which is where Larry came in, and me along with him riding shotgun, offering them a couple of bob to spend on sweets, or to light multiple candles in the cathedral like His Holiness Stephen Gilmartin, who Maura said had declared himself Pope in 1959. There was four of them we generally dealt with, and they were religious maniacs to a man.

Anyhow, we did well that day, a haul of four tidy lumps of plug with money left over for us. Larry had a mind then to stay in town and go to the pictures. He said there were nudies in the film that was showing and he was determined to try and see them. I pleaded that the folks would miss me if I wasn't back by teatime but he was having none of it, said

I was just a scaredy. Which was pretty much the truth of it, in all fairness. So we parted, anyhow, and I set off for home alone, taking the long way in order to mull things over, which is how I came to pass Monksfield House.

Monksfield was a big fancy two-story house that'd belonged to a Captain Angel, who'd been in the British Army. He was Protestant, and when he died there was a big row over who in the family should get it, so it'd been vacant for quite a while. But it was vacant no longer, a brand-new Wolseley 16/60 parked outside it, and in the field out the back, a boy at something, I couldn't see what. So, I left me bike on the ditch and crawled up to have a gawk.

He was kneeling, fiddling with something on the ground, but then he stood and I saw what it was, because he launched it out of his hand, the biggest, best model aeroplane I'd ever seen. And did it fly, up into the sky, and round the field, and him running after it like a madman. Ages, it stayed up. It was nothing like the rubbishy little things that came in Lucky Bags that broke after about two flights, if you were lucky. This was the real thing. I would've loved to have got a closer look, but as ever I was too shy, so I stayed put and just watched. He flew it a couple more times, then his ma or someone called him and he went inside. I headed home determined to rustle up Larry the next morning. Because though Larry was a lot of things, shy wasn't one of them.

The mystery of the new tenants of Monksfield lasted all of an hour after I'd got home.

'Wait until I tell yiz.' It seemed our new neighbour was none other than the boss of the whole Mental, Dr Hyland. 'He's a gentleman, the best resident medical superintendent in the country.' Except he was resident no longer because the family quarters in the Mental were being done up.

'Does he have family?' the ma asked.

'He does, one wife and one son,' Maura said. 'I do see the lad, he's Danny's age. It must be a quare old life for him, locked up inside those walls with all the carry-on. Sure he couldn't be right.'

'And he's up at Monksfield now?' the ma says and looks at me. 'There'd be a grand pal for you now, Danny, instead of that little latchiko Larry MacGowan.' She never had a good word for poor Larry. I suppose there was a bit of a snob in her, because as little as we had, the MacGowan's had less. And she never tired of reminding us, the da and me, that his granny had been born 'under the canvas.'

'And sure what if she was,' the da would say. 'Aren't the tinkers people too?' That was the thing about the da, he wouldn't hear a bad word said against anyone. Straight, I suppose you'd call it. Or simple, the ma would say when her dander was up.

Anyhow, next morning I was down to Larry's first thing. Now y'never knew what was going to greet you at the MacGowans, whether it was Mrs MacGowan hitching up her blouse to put yet another baby on, or her husband PJ snoring on the couch in his drawers after a big feed of porter. This particular morning, I was wary because the last time, Larry's next older sister Francie had taken to doing handstands in front of me.

'Don't mind her, Danny,' Larry explained, 'Mammy's only after buying her a bra and she's showing it off.' The fact was I was nearly fourteen at this stage. It might sound like a big age to be still in national school, but me and Larry and some of the country children were in seventh-class because we weren't going to secondary school, so we had to stay on and sit for our Primary Certificate and maybe get a scholarship. Except Larry swore blind he was sitting no exams at all. 'I'm going to end up driving a shovel for the County Council just like Daddy and divil a certificate I need to do that.' I was of the same mind, except I'd be driving my shovel for CIE, but the ma was very insistent I go for the scholarship. She never gave me a minute's peace about lessons and homework.

'Hello missus. We'd like to talk to the boy with the aeroplane,' Larry beamed up at the woman who'd answered his very loud knock. She smiled back. She was tall and had her hair done up, and wore a flowery dress.

'Tarran is gone swimming, actually. He's just down there,' she pointed.

'Thanks, missus,' Larry gave her a big thumbs-up. She grinned, watched us leave, only closing the door when we were back out onto the road. 'Did you see the big diddies on her?' Larry could say anything, and generally did.

'Jazes Larry,' I laughed.

'And Tarran? What sort of a fuckin' name is Tarran?'

'Don't fuckin' know.' We all used bad language all the time. In descending order of popularity, fuck, hoor, cunt, bollix. The da never ever used bad words, so I wasn't the worst when it came down to it. And funnily enough, I remember never swearing when I was in Tarran's company.

He was out of the sea and towelling himself down that day. My height, a big head of blondy curls, and it was funny him just stood there in his trunks and us dressed. For all that we lived beside the sea we had no interest in it. If cousins visited from up the country we'd go to the beach, and naturally the place was full of holidaymakers in the summer. But living there was no holiday, and we mostly turned our backs on it.

'I'm Larry and this is Danny.'

'Pleased to meet you, I'm Tarran,' he said, and fuck me if he didn't hold out his hand and we both had to shake it.

'We're sorry for your troubles,' Larry said and I burst out laughing. I could see he probably thought we were a right pair of goms so I stepped in and explained about the plane and how we'd love to see it. He was agreeable, so off the three of us back to the house where his ma let us in and told us we'd have to take our shoes off if we wanted to go any further. Nice and polite though, not like Nancy Hart, Noel's mother, who'd let out a scream at you if you got mud on her lino. The Harts had a big guesthouse in the village, and Nancy was very house-proud and particular. Or as Larry had it, a right cunt altogether.

Big as the Hart's place was, Monksfield was far grander and me and Larry were all eyes as we went up the massive staircase, our toes out through our socks, nails snagging on the carpets. We'd never seen such luxury – big mirrors with gold frames on the wall, and paintings of horses, and vases on cabinets, and glass fronted cupboards full of silver. Tarran's bedroom was bigger than our kitchen and front-room put together.

He got the plane out and showed it to us. Larry asked could he hold it and he passed it over. But then Larry went to launch it across the room and he had to grab it back off him.

'Don't be a twit, it'll smash itself against the wall,' he said and we all laughed. Larry had never been called a twit before and it just seemed funny. After that he showed us where he was building another, on a board, with the plans laid out and the little bits of wood pinned down to make up the spars and ribs.

'Can we go out and fly one?' Larry didn't have much interest in the plans and the glue and the little bits of balsa wood. He could never sit still for long, that was Larry.

'I'm afraid it's too windy today,' Tarran said, and he must

have seen how disappointed we were, because next thing he was on his knees getting a box out from under his bead. 'Look at this. I'm going to set it up on that table over there and make scenery.' It was a trainset – tracks, points, signals, a black steam locomotive and four goods wagons. My eyes fair lit up. And when Larry piped up how the da was a railway man, Tarran began bombarding me with questions. I'd picked up a lot of talk and words and procedures from listening to the da down the years and I had him hanging on my every word. He was mad interested in trains, and I suppose I was myself, it being what we did, the Freynes. Even if it was just shovelling ballast out of a pile and throwing it between the sleepers.

Anyhow, Larry soon got bored listening to us and suggested we head back into the village for a game of soccer. Tarran said he never got to play soccer because he went to the Christian Brothers and asked could he tag along. So off with the three of us. There were usually enough around to cobble some sort of match together, even if it was just a game of three-goals-in. There was Noel Hart and his little brother Tommy. Finbar Conlon and his brother Mickey, and an even smaller one, Joe. Connie O'Hara could kick a ball, so could Larry's next younger sister Peg, and Rose Hegarty would agree to do goal as long as no one shouted at her. There were usually a couple more, and this particular day we had a right good match because having Tarran seemed to balance the numbers better. He was on our team and we ended up beating Finbar's team ten-nine.

After that we just sat around, asked Tarran questions about living in the Mental, and who was the maddest madman in it, and what was the maddest thing he'd seen happen, and was it true that they all went loo-la when there was a full moon. Which he didn't have answers for a lot of, though he did agree that Pope Stephen Gilmartin was 'very bonkers altogether.' Then we quizzed him up on his school, and what sort of weaponry the Brothers used, and he explained it was a short length of leather, a strap doubled back on itself, with stitching down each side which left its print in your hand when you got it.

'And do you get it much?' Finbar asked him like he didn't believe he ever got it at all. Because he was like that, Finbar, a sort of know-all and a jeer at the same time. Tarran said that he did, often enough. 'What did you do, so, the last time then?' Finbar challenged him, and it was true he did seem to struggle to come up with something. Eventually he said he'd left his homework copy back at home, and it got him three on each hand.

'Every spring when the buds are on the ash, the Master cuts himself a supply of rods and stores them up. The buds do bring you out in welts,' I wiggled my fingers.

'And does he hit the girls too?' Tarran asked.

'No, he gets Mrs Reid to do it, the bitch,' Connie said and we all laughed and Tarran turned a bit red. Connie was in seventh class along with me and Larry.

After that Noel and Finbar started quizzing Tarran about his dad's Wolseley and how fast it could go. The Hart's had an Anglia and the Conlons had a Cortina. We had no car at all of course, just the da's Honda Fifty that he went to work on. And the MacGowans just had their feet. Needless to say, Finbar insisted that the Cortina was faster than the Wolseley because anything the Conlons had was better than what anyone else had. Finbar's da owned a drapers in Sligo and employed five people to run it. They went on holidays every summer and Finbar would come back and tell us stories about things he'd seen and done that none of us believed, though we let on we did.

The rain came on then. Larry volunteered to show Tarran his pet rabbit, so we wandered over towards his place. On the way, Larry ducked into the lane behind Dwyer's, their dog started barking and there was shouts, and he tore back out again holding a bunch of cabbage leaves. 'Run!' he shouted and the three of us tore of down the street laughing.

Everyone at MacGowan's was sort of dumbstruck at the sight of Tarran, the little ones stopping fighting just to stare, Francie open-mouthed and speechless, too surprised to even think about showing off her new bra. We went out the back and fed the leaves to the rabbit and they all looked on. I suppose he was a bit of a sight, Tarran, with the big blondy curly head, but he had a sort of way with him, ever so polite, but easy with people too, grownups included. When we eventually decided to go, I had to wait ages for him outside the house because he got talking to Mrs MacGowan.

'It's different here to town,' he said on our way home.

'How so?'

'Dunno. It's all a big mill of kids every age. And girls kicking football. Y'wouldn't see that in town.'

'There's only us here and we have to make do, I suppose.'

'Nahh, I like it,' he said, and then we fell to talking about the railways again, and detonators in particular that the permanent way men would put out to warn of an approaching train. I told him I might be able to get one off the da, and he was thrilled. I didn't think I would of course, because they were explosive and the da was very cagey with that sort of thing.

It rained for the rest of the holidays. Most days I went up to Tarran's and we worked on the model railway. I got bits of lichen and moss and we made trees with it. Tarran had a cardboard box and we made a tunnel out of that, covering it with paper and glue and painting it green like it was grass. A couple of times when I went home the ma told me Larry had called to see where I was, and I could see how pleased she was that she could tell him I was up at Monksfield. He hadn't come up either, which was a bit strange because usually we did everything together. I didn't think much about it at the time, though, because Larry was well able to amuse himself.

Then it was back to school. It was a bit different this time because we knew it was our last term. Much and all as we hated school I suppose deep down we realized that once it was over, real grown-up life would begin. And for me anyway, that didn't look like a lot of fun. Larry was different, he couldn't wait to escape from sums and reading and Irish, couldn't wait to be earning some money for himself. But I was sad going back, thinking how it was all coming to an end.

Another thing that was more obvious was the differences between us all, where we came from, where we were going. Up to then we'd been all together, us against the teachers, against grownups in general. But now the likes of Finbar and Noel, and Tarran indeed, were heading off to secondary school, the rest of us just mucking around like our sort of people always did.

Another difference, that last term, was that Tarran was in the class. It was actually kinda good because me and Larry were his buddies, we hung around together at playtime, and it ranked us up in the eyes of the country kids. Tarran was a novelty, and even the Master behaved sort of different to him, the way he spoke. Of course, Tarran was bright, anyone could see that.

It wasn't all plain sailing though. Finbar Conlon in

particular took a scunner against him, probably because he was jealous that he wasn't top dog any longer. Anyhow, one day an argument started in the yard over whether Tarran's da was a doctor or not. Finbar insisted that he wasn't and of course Tarran said he was, that he was a psychiatric doctor. And Finbar said no, doctors cured people who were sick, who had diseases. Mad people were just mad, and didn't have diseases, and so it wasn't a doctor who looked after them.

'But there are diseases, and conditions,' Tarran insisted. 'Like Down syndrome. You get born with it. Like Larry's Uncle Mick. He was born with it, and he has to be in the Mental so he can be looked after.' Of course at this Larry turned bright pink because we'd never heard of this Uncle Mick.

'Y'mean, Larry has an uncle who's an imbecile?' Finbar guffawed, and so did Noel, and everyone started laughing at Larry.

'Fuck yiz all,' Larry shouted, 'fuck yiz,' and off he was gone, out of the school yard and away down the road.

'Imbecile, Micky, Micky, Micky, Micky,' Finbar shouted after him. Tarran was looking kinda sick, realizing what he'd done, but it was too late now. On the way home that evening he explained that he knew Mrs MacGowan from her visiting her brother. I told him he needed to go and apologise to Larry and down we went the pair of us there and then. At first Larry wouldn't even come out, and when he did he'd hardly look at us. Tarran said his piece, how he was sorry, and that he hadn't understood. I kinda spoke up for him and eventually Larry softened, said it was alright. But I knew it wasn't really. Larry would have to put up with an awful lot of extra guff at school. But that was just the way of it, y'had to carry on with things, swallow what couldn't be spat out.

Eventually the weather picked up. And after all the rain it seemed like it might be a good time to go fishing. It was the da who'd showed me and Larry how to fish the little bog river that wove back inland through the rushes and bogs and forestry. Where the best spots were, and how you had to be really quiet what with the boggy banks quaking when you walked on them and frightening off the trout. The trout were small, tiny really, but two would make a really sweet breakfast. Part of fishing was digging for worms, and we'd be thrilled if we got one of the black-headed lads, because everyone knew that these were the ones the trout liked the best.

So in the evenings, instead of football, a gang of us would head up the river. The usual squad was me, Larry, Finbar, Noel, Connie, Peg, Rose sometimes, and sometimes someone's little brother. No matter what kind of rows we'd had during the day at school they all got forgotten with and off we'd go with our rods and our cans of worms. And now we had Tarran along as well.

Of course, there was more messing than fishing done a lot of the time. And if the trout were scared by the banks quaking, then we must have frightened the bejeesus out of them regularly. There'd be teasing and all kinds of carry-on. One time Larry put a worm down his sister's back, another time Noel caught a frog and chased Rose half-way home threatening to put it down her knickers.

Anyway, it came to this one particular evening, a Wednesday I think, and it was really hot and muggy. We were a long way up the river, up in the plantation where there was a bit of shade from the sun. The only problem was the flies and the midges driving us crazy. We had out shirts off, swinging them over our heads to keep them off. It was only Connie and Rose with us that evening, and as usual the messing started.

And as usual the rack was between Connie and Finbar, them swapping insults and pushing each other around. Anyhow, this time they got really thick with each other and a sort of wrestling match developed, and next thing Connie calls Rose in to help her, and then Noel is grabbing at Rose and the four of them are in a tangle. Then Finbar sticks his head up out of it and calls over to me and Larry and Tarran.

'Hey lads, let's strip them,' he shouts and next thing he has Connie's blouse up over her head. Meself and Tarran are rooted to the spot, but not Larry, he wades into it, and suddenly there's vests and skirts and knickers and socks flying every which way. I suppose transfixed is what we were, me and Tarran. And of course we couldn't look away, seeing things we'd never seen before, and how Connie had hair and Rose didn't, and breasts too, where Rose hardly had any. I suppose I was thinking of Larry's sister, how she wanted me to see her bra. I was a biteen slow for my years, on this front, no doubt about it. But that was all changed now.

And then it broke up, the lads stood up and stepped back, kinda grinning, but kinda shocked too, and a bit sheepish. The two girls grabbed for their clothes and covered themselves up again. Rose was crying but Connie was just red with rage. Not shouty rage, just angry with mortification, I suppose, that she'd let Finbar best her. She told Rose to stop snivelling and go check on their rods which were round the bend of the river.

After that we just did some more fishing. I caught a baby pike which we'd never seen the like of before in the river, but the fun was kinda gone out of the evening and we knocked off soon after. There was a bit of back-and forth between Connie and Finbar, a bit of name-calling, but just the usual bickering they gave each other. Eventually it was just me and Larry and Tarran heading back our road.

'Some diddies on Connie, all the same,' Larry gave a laugh.

'It wasn't right what ye did,' Tarran muttered.

'Sure it was just messin'.'

'Rose is just a child, more or less.'

'Well sure we couldn't strip Connie and not strip her. That would have left her out, which wouldn't have been fair.'

'Are you serious?'

'I am,' Larry grinned to me, 'deadly serious.'

'He's not, he's only messing,' I said. Tarran wasn't at all impressed. After we'd left Larry he said it again to me, how it wasn't right what'd happened. I tried to explain how Connie and Finbar had been at odds since second-class, that they couldn't leave the other alone. But he wasn't having it. He made a fist of one hand and bashed it into his other.

'It just wasn't right.'

I hadn't seen this stubborn side to him before, so I gave up on it. It seemed when he got his mind set on something there was no changing it.

It was odd, but the next day in school at break, Noel said something about fishing, were we going, and I said I was, and Connie said she was, and so did Larry, and so that evening the same gang up the river, Finbar, Tarran, Rose, all of us. We were all a bit skittish and a lot of messing, and I suppose at the back of our minds was the question whether it was all going to kick off again. But it didn't, we just fished mostly, though Connie and Finbar did get into another tussle at some point. Tarran was very quiet though.

When it was just me and him and Larry on the way home he started up on it again, how it wasn't right what'd happened. Eventually Larry lost his patience.

'Would you ever stop going on about it. You didn't do

anything to stop us. And I saw y'looking too. So don't come over all holy with me.'

This didn't quieten Tarran.

'It was still wrong.'

Then Larry got a kind of a glint in his eye, gave a bit of a guffaw.

'You're sweet on Connie, aren't you. That's it Danny, our Tarran is sweet on Connie, so he is. That's what it is.' He laughed and laughed.

'Ah jazzes Larry, don't start up on that shite,' I said and he turned on me.

'What's it to you, y'feckin' gobdaw,' he said, and he meant it too. It was the first truly bitter word he'd ever aimed in my direction, and he didn't stick around after saying it either, which left me feeling none too good. I knew what it was, of course – he felt left out, me hanging round so much with Tarran. When Tarran started giving out about what'd happened yet again, I didn't have a lot of patience with him.

'Well why did Connie come back out this evening?' I said. 'And Rose too. If it was all so terrible. Why?' But he wasn't having it, there was no talking to him. And there was worse to come.

I suppose I don't blame Larry, but obviously he hadn't really forgiven Tarran for spilling the beans on his Uncle Micky. By lunch break the next day it was gone around the whole school that Tarran Hyland was sweet on Connie O'Hara, that they were going to get married and have five children, and live in the Mental. And a lot more teasing besides, like always happened in these situations. Except Tarran wasn't used to it and was mortified. It didn't help that his future wife said he was a soft eejit and that she'd rather marry Larry's Uncle Micky.

This was a Friday. Saturday afternoon I went down to Monksfield as usual, but this time his ma told me Tarran wasn't there, that he was gone off doing stuff with his da. Even though their car was still there in the yard. I suppose I should have guessed something was up, but I didn't. It was only Monday morning when I saw Fr Mannion's Ford Popular parked outside the school, and met Noel Hart, his face white as a sheet, that I copped it. Tarran had shopped us.

Even now the memory of it makes my blood run cold, the shame, the humiliation. Fr Mannion interrogated us one by one, who did what, who started it, who was to blame, got us all to turn on each other. By the end of it we hardly knew our names. Then there was the confessions and the penances that went on for hours.

We were denounced from the altar, not by name of course, but everyone knew. Sins of the flesh, purity, Satan waiting to lead us astray. And he came round to our houses, left the ma wailing and screeching about the disgrace of it all, the da sad as sad could be. She made him give me a beating me with a belt, except he didn't really, a few half-hearted whacks on me shins, that was it, and him nearly in tears. I was in tears meself, fourteen though I was.

I have no recollection of the last few weeks of national school. I must have done the Primary Certificate exams I suppose, and needless to say there was no scholarship for me. It was then that a rare occurrence happened, me ma and Maura fell into unanimous agreement, which was never a good thing for the men in our house. They said I'd never come to any good if I stayed put, that there'd been too much talk, that I had a reputation now. So, I was to be shipped up to their brother John who lived on the Navan Road in Dublin and start as carpenter's apprentice with him. I was to be got out of

Dodge, plain and simple. The da was heartbroken. I suppose he had dreams of meself and himself heading off together for a pint on a Friday evening after the week's work on the rails, pals as ever. But it wasn't to be. He did put the foot down on one thing – I was to be no carpenter. He got on to the assistant stationmaster Sam Collingwood who he was friendly with, and he moved heaven and earth and got me the start at the Inchicore Works. The Freynes were railway men and that was it. Good and all as this was, I was a still a sad lonely boy facing off into the unknown at the end of that June.

Tarran never came back to the school. I only saw him the once after, on the road, he was on his way for a swim. Why did you do it, I asked him, and I could see he was a bit shook after what'd we'd all been put through. All except him, of course. But still he came out with the same line. He said he'd told his ma, and his ma said it was wrong, and that with his da being what he was, he would have to tell what happened. And sure what could I say. That his ma and da didn't know Finbar and Connie? That his da didn't know priests? That they didn't understand anything at all?

Anyhow, it was all this that filled my head as I took the return service back to Connolly that evening after Feeney told me. I'd known Larry was gone a bit off the rails, had gotten arrested for thieving, was on the bottle a lot. And I felt bad at how I'd let things slip between us, which I had. Because I owed him a lot when it came down to it. If it hadn't been for the street-schooling he gave me I might not have thrived up in Dublin the way I did.

Needless to say, it was him that'd come out the worst after what'd happened. Finbar and Noel hadn't suffered much of a set-back at all, had done their Leaving, one now a big business-man, the other a hotel-manager. Immediately after,

Connie had gotten shipped off to work for nuns in a laundry, but it wasn't long before she went over the wall and took off for London. She hadn't been heard of since. Rose was gone strange, a bit Church-mad like the ma, spending her days praying and doing devotions. But really it was Larry who'd taken the fall for all of us. And now he was in the Mental along with his Uncle Micky. Wasn't it just the way things worked out.

It must have been five years after that again, me and Nancy were expecting our first, so 1979, I suppose. I was on the 18:10 service for Sligo and hadn't got far beyond the Clonsilla Box when a serious over-heat started to build. Those re-engined Metrovicks were never quite right, too much of a power mis-match. Anyhow, I nursed her into Maynooth and we laid up there to wait for the relief engine to come out.

It must have been summer, because it was a fine evening, and I was out of the cab, kicking me heels, having a smoke, when I see a figure across from me on the far platform. A fine big shape of a man in priestly garb, blondy head on him, very dapper indeed. Tarran Hyland. Fr. Tarran Hyland, I suppose. And it all came back to me again, what'd happened. Only by now Larry was dead three years. Feeney didn't have his wish, he was out of the Mental after a only a few months, but he was never right after. Eventually he went into the Garvoge and it was a month or two before he was found, body washed up out at Oyster Island.

So all this is running through my head as I look over at him. And damn me, I don't know if I should make myself known to him or not. Talk to him, tell him how I felt about what'd happened, what he'd done. As if I knew what I felt. Me, I was a respected man, well liked, his own house and a family on the way. He'd done me no harm in the long run.

But Larry? Connie? Rose even? I didn't know the hell. In the end I let him be, none the wiser. What was to be gained by doing otherwise, for him or for me. Nothing, as far as I could see. I might have done it for Larry, I suppose. But really, if anyone had let Larry down it was me, his closest friend, not Tarran Hyland.

Grit. It'd just be a handful of grit thrown in his face. Because that's the way I've come to look back on it now, after all the years. That there's a weight to living in this world and you carry it like your pockets are full of grit. There's some people, a lot, who do their damnedest just to get rid of it, flinging it here and flinging it there, not giving a damn. That's the majority. Then there's the likes of a Tarran Hyland, who think there must be some purpose to having it. Who start scattering it where they think it'll do some good. Giving someone traction, or stopping them from sliding away. But is it really the thing to do – that's what I'd like to know. Would it not be better, maybe, if people just kept their hands out of their pockets altogether, got resigned to carrying the weight themselves. Like I carry the memory of poor Larry, how I forged on while he went off the rails. Ballast for the conscience, is what it really is.

2: 1978

SHAUN

'Mom said you couldn't land without anyone being here to meet you ...' Ed's words too fast, his smile too wide, that bearhug an unknown quantity. Travis men don't do overt expressions of affection and Ed and I are not huggers, or weren't, until now.

'Good to have you home, bro.'

Ed's accent is pure north-west Ireland, while mine is more a mishmash of America, Ireland and after three years away, I guess some London sneaking in there too.

'Assigned to escort duty, Ed?' I return his hug with a brief squeeze, disentangle myself.

Both of us aware he's only here because of Mom. She knows me well enough to guess I'd try to bottle out of this trip, and she was right. Mid-air, I was planning to hop the next plane back to Heathrow, say I missed my flight.

'She's taking no chances,' he says, reading my mind with a grin that if I didn't know better, I'd call verging on self-conscious. Never one of Ed's traits: with him, you get what you see.

And what I'm seeing is not the kid brother I left behind. The long, loose limbs have anchored into place, his face settled into a late teen version of Dad. Same shaggy dark hair too, reined in today, almost tidy. Longish, hooked nose, another Travis trademark.

'Mom has a shift at the hospital and Dad's on a deadline, otherwise they'd be here themselves,' his voice deliberately light.

Shifts and deadlines, tell me something new. A veteran of the Vietnam war, Dad's a freelance journalist, been published in The New Yorker and National Geographic. Mom's a trauma care nurse. They fell for each other in the Casualty Department of Boston General right after Dad had another kind of fall, off his Kawasaki 750. He shipped the bike from the States when we moved here. Mom used to say he loved it more than he loved her. Don't think that was true, but probably a close-run thing.

'So ... still trying to save the house from sliding into the sea?'

'That's about right,' and this time the grin is wide open.

Which makes me smile, too. We share a close acquaintance with draughts, mould and damp courtesy of Monksfield House. Mom's dream of returning home from Boston morphed into Dad's dream of living in a place with history sewn into its seams. Over the years, he's blown every cent he inherited from his own father on keeping the leaky, stone pile in the neighbourhood of habitable.

I pitch my rucksack in Ed's direction, he makes a fake lunge. Catches my eye as he straightens up, a question there. Trying to figure out my mood. How I'm going to play this, what to say, what to leave out. Whether to broach the subject we've avoided for three years.

As he hefts the rucksack, I do a double take, 'Is that my jacket?'

'Yeah, figured you didn't need it anymore, bro. What do you think?' Twisting to give me a better view of the faded denim with the patches of Bowie and Deep Purple, stitched on painfully by yours truly. The jacket I was wearing the day Ella and I got together and the night Aidan died.

As Ed spins round, I notice something else. Someone else. A girl. Hanging back, looking out from behind Ed's shoulder. Fair hair tumbled around a familiar face. Blue eyes, dark lashes. Looking at me. My heart so loud in my ears that tannoy announcements and passing conversations fall away. Our eyes lock, familiar in an unfamiliar way. Plunging me into memories of someone else.

She shoots Ed a smile, sweet and questioning all at once, enough to tip me over. I grab my brother, drag him aside, 'What the fuck do you think you're doing?'

He jerks out of my grip, reaches for her, a protectiveness that screams something that's been happening for a while. A stubborn look from childhood frames his face, 'Look, Sarah and me, we wanted to be upfront from the start, this has nothing to do with you, or Ella …'

I'm staring at him. Of all the scenarios playing out in my head about what coming home might look like, none featured Ed waiting at the airport with Ella's sister. Ella's sister. I shake my head, then turn towards the exit.

'Where's the car? And I want my denim back, you fucking moron.'

It's a three-hour journey. Hunched in the back of Dad's Citroën Dyane, I blank out Ed's attempts at small talk. Powder coated fields fly past. Winter snow. White, almost blinding. A softer landscape than the one I left in January

1976 when the Big Storm was on the way out, mangled trees, flooded rivers tracking its retreat.

My instinct was right, I shoulda stayed in London, same as last year: a visit to aunt Irene, and her husband, Ian, in Finsbury Park, maybe hit a party with the guys from work another night, then some downtime in my bedsit over the café. Festive fare, mostly on my own, and that's not me complaining, just the way it needs to be. What I deserve.

If it hadn't been for Mom's call, two weeks out from Christmas, a Friday night, her usual time, that's how it woulda played out. Truth is, I hadn't slept much the night before, too many dreams slipping into nightmares so I was easy prey and she boxed me into a corner before I knew it.

'It won't be a celebration without you, Shaun. How can we have a party knowing you're on your own in London?'

'When is it?'

'New Year's Eve. Dad wants it to be the exact date of our wedding.' She was quiet for a second, then, 'I know, the day before Aidan's anniversary, which isn't ideal, but … '

And there it was. The thing Mom and Dad tiptoe around, refer to obliquely. The thing Ed and I have never mentioned, not once, since I left. Aidan's crash. Aidan's smash, Aidan's accident. And now, Aidan's anniversary. Not their fault, I've become pretty good at shutting people down.

Things might have been different if I hadda shut Aidan down from the first day in school. Yeah, if only.

So, I'm not saying this is how it was or anything, just that there mighta been a part of me relieved to feel I had no choice. That I had to be there, for them, do something right, for once. Anyhow, before I could stop myself, the words were out, 'Okay, Mom, I'll be there, wouldn't miss it.'

Three years older than me, Aidan was beefy, big hands, big bones, even bigger mouth. I was lanky, not much into fighting. And there was always the Mom thing. Aidan was my aunt Maura's eldest of six kids. Mom is fond of her older sister, not so much her husband, Jack. If I'd known what volatile meant back then, that's the word I woulda used for him. Loud, like Aidan. Rough around the edges is what Mom said, guess she had a hunch Jack made it more complicated than that.

Something to notice, Mom tends to dress things up, as in when she discovered Aidan was already attending my new primary school, not something I got the feeling she was pumped about, but still tried to spin. 'Look, Shaun, having Aidan there for your first year will make it easier to fit in, he'll look after you.'

Now it just seems dumb to expect that because Aidan and I were related, we could ever be friends.

I was fourth class to his sixth and my American twang marked me out, that and the crap about my name, even from the teacher. From day one, Aidan made it his business to assume the role of minder, 'Lads, leave the cousin alone. It's not his fault he talks funny and can't spell.'

Not that he was any kind of scholar and even to my kid's ears, signalling my differences didn't seem designed to help me fit in. And it was shaming, the other boys thinking I needed to hide behind my big cousin.

Didn't take long to realise Aidan had his own interpretation of 'minding.'

'Anyone messes with the yank, messes with me.'

As he said that, he stretched out a leg to trip me. I hit the concrete in the yard, face first, still remember the shock. Calculated to make me look stupid. Anyway, the message went out. I was protected, but not from Aidan.

I couldn't avoid him, he was always there, at the gate before school, during breaks, after school, keen to devote special attention to me. 'What's for lunch today, Shaunie,' grabbing my school bag, meaty fingers digging through whatever Mom put in my lunchbox. Sharing it with his moron friends, each delighted not to be me.

Shaunie. Making me more of a school joke than I was already.

Mom was on the receiving end of a lot of lies that first year. Lies to excuse the bruises, the stolen sports gear, the torn books. I could hardly tell her that her nephew was a psychopath, not that I knew that word either back then, just a fair idea of what it looked like. And then there was my spectacular fail in making friends, which worried her, but wasn't surprising when you factor in that no-one wanted to take my place in Aidan's affections.

Dad didn't notice. His job in 'Nam had been to write up the action, not be part of it, but I guess he saw stuff there which sometimes sent him somewhere in his head we couldn't go. He'd lock himself in the study and not long after, a sickly-sweet smell would snake out from under the door, Mom's cue to protect me and Ed from something she figured we didn't need to know. 'Leave your Dad in peace. He needs time to find himself.'

I worried about Dad. If he was truly lost, if he'd ever be able to find his way back. I guess my worst fear was that someone different would emerge from the study. But after a day or so, we'd wake up one morning and he'd be there, in the kitchen, frying eggs, taking orders for his special pancakes, maple syrup and bacon. Haggard, yellowish, shaky, but still Dad.

So, yeah, he had enough going on in his head, I was never going to talk to him about Aidan.

It was like being released from jail when Aidan left primary school, except by then he'd started spending time at ours. Mom said we needed to be kind to him, treated him like a lost sheep. And to be fair, he put on a good show, disguised the sneer when the parents were around. Had Dad fooled. Aidan was the only one who got to help him strip the bike down, put it back together. Watching them get tight was tough to take.

Seems strange now I never wondered why Aidan wanted to be at our place so much. Guess I put it down to him always wanting what I had.

Ed's voice nudges me back to the car, something about our old school's rugby team. I'm still ignoring him, so he shrugs, sends a reassuring smile to Sarah, then turns up the radio. They keep their conversation low, barely audible under the post-Christmas chat of the local station. Can't resist a quick glance. Six years younger than Ella, long hair, pushed back behind her ears, curve of her lips visible from the side, smatter of freckles on her cheek. She could be Ella, but she's not. I could be Shaun, but I guess that's not a given either.

Ella's family, the Conlons, own a drapery shop in the centre of town, have always had more money than most and figure they're a touch above the rest. I had a crush on her since … well, I'll say twelve, but if I'm being honest, even before that.

Mostly, she blanked me in class, same as she did the other boys, but sometimes if she glanced back to where I was sitting our eyes would catch, sending my stomach into freefall.

After primary, I headed off to boarding school in Dublin, Ella to the local Convent Secondary. I didn't see her again until after I was expelled. That happened when a tin box with some spliffs was discovered in my laundry bag after the Easter holidays of Second Year. The Head wanted me to explain how, if the box wasn't mine, it came to be in my bag, but I was hardly going to squeal on Dad.

Packed off on the train from Heuston with a letter setting out the reasons for my expulsion, I shredded it just outside Maynooth. A wasted effort, because the Head phoned ahead to warn the parents I was on my way.

'Well, Shaunie, that's a tough break, but a bit stupid to steal your Dad's stash, wouldn't you think?'

Aidan's gloating grin a few days later confirmed something I'd suspected … that he'd been the one to fuck me over. Thanks to him, I now trailed the whiff of being some kind of junkie while the folks scrambled to find a school willing to accept me.

'You think taking drugs will help you get on in life?'

It was early April, Mom still trying to come to terms with what she termed 'Shaun's disgrace.' As well as dressing stuff up, she has a knack for calling it.

'Look, Mom, for the last time, I don't take drugs, the box wasn't mine, and I didn't put it in my laundry bag. Anyway, Dad smokes dope, what's the big deal?'

The look on her face, as if I'd slapped her.

Dad came into the kitchen in time to hear and any last hope he might admit it was his stash, that he didn't believe I'd stolen it, evaporated when he said, 'Do as I say, Shaun, not as I do,' the words out as easily as if he'd been rehearsing them.

And maybe that was my moment to tell the parents my fall from grace was down to golden boy, Aidan, but like Dad, something held me back. Pride, I guess. I mean, this was my Dad, it was his job to be on my side. He shoulda known Aidan was playing him. That I wasn't a thief. Whatever.

Later that day, I was rambling through town, head down, thinking up ways to get even. Didn't notice two girls in convent school uniform coming towards me.

My arm grazed off the girl closest to me and heat rose to my face as I met her amused, blue-eyed gaze, 'Oh, sorry, I didn't mean ... '

'No problem,' she shrugged, started to move away.

'Ella?'

She turned back, looked me up and down and I waited for her to blank me, same as always.

'Shaun? Or should I say Shaunie?'

I felt my face flush.

'Ha, ha ... no-one calls me that, only Aidan ... ' I tailed off.

'I know,' she replied, 'And I often wondered why you were cool with it.'

'With what?' Regretting the question as soon as it was out.

'Him making fun of you, trying to make you seem like a nobody.'

By then, word was out I'd been kicked out of school, which for some meant I was someone to avoid and for others, made me cool. Turned out Ella hadn't heard any of it, but when I told her my side, she believed me.

'So, to sum up, snowstorms will be more extensive inland, while coastal areas are likely to see an increase in rain with some wind, though not gale force levels.'

I've just listened to the entire farming forecast from Radio West, the familiar inflections heightening the feeling since getting home yesterday that I've stepped back in time. Every room and cupboard reeks of the same damp I grew up with, the same grey roar of the sea leaking through the walls of the old house.

I edge back the frayed net curtains over the kitchen sink. Mom's vegetable garden, smudged in what Dad calls 'a perpetual mist,' edged by trees blown into eerie shapes by a westerly breeze. When he's in a good mood, usually defined by whether the words are going onto the page, he's likely to call the rain 'the curtain between here and somewhere else.' As if there's anything magical about the weather. Otherwise, it's 'this fucking piss pot of a country.'

But at least Dad won't wanna get into some deep and meaningful discussion about how I'm feeling, how I'm doing, that no-one blames me, it wasn't my fault, all crap that's not true, means nothing.

I don't notice he's come into the kitchen until he says, 'Ah, Shaun, thought I might find you here.'

His hair, still thick, barely any grey, stands in tufts on his head, a sludge brown cardigan I'd swear he was wearing in 1976 hanging loose over a creased linen shirt and grey trousers. He looks tired, a little neglected.

And then I can't help it, have to smile. The man who survived 'Nam and a motorbike smash, the man who couldn't live in Ireland without his Kawasaki, the coolest dude I've ever known, is wearing purple, plush velvet slippers.

Dad shakes his head, grins, 'I know, old man apparel, Shaun. A present from your mom for Christmas, how can I not wear them?'

'You could pretend to lose them,' I suggest, 'Or say the dog ate them?'

'If we had a dog,' he laughs, reaching for the coffee percolator on the shelf beside the Aga. 'Want some?'

'Sure, count me in.'

Watching him scoop coffee, I say, 'Everything looks the same as when I left …' I break off.

'It's not, though, is it?'

And there goes my theory about deep and meaningful. Dad's voice is raw, he's avoiding my eyes. How could I have ever imagined he'd tell me it wasn't my fault, when of course he blames me. He and Aidan were close, spent hours together, bonded over their love of the bike. Dad never saw the Aidan I knew, only a curated version.

'Shaun, there's something I need to say, something I shoulda said before …'

I can't look at him. Don't think I can bear to hear what he's gonna to say. I've been telling myself I'm beyond this, beyond feeling as if my chest is being squeezed through a strainer. That the more I repeat I'm fine, I'm over it, the more that becomes the truth. But repeating something doesn't work that kind of miracle.

Dad puts the percolator on the stove, turns back to me slowly, 'It's my fault you were thrown out of school, if I hadn't had the weed, there would have been no problem,' he shakes his head, 'I'm sorry, Shaun, I let you down.'

When I was a kid, and before I understood Dad better, he was the hero of every crudely drawn battle in the Hotspur and Victor comics. Then, I guess I was about ten, I asked him how many of the enemy he'd killed in battle.

'Killing isn't something to boast about, Shaun,' his voice icy. 'Travis men are army men, that's the mantra I grew up with. Well, that's just not true. You can be anything you wanna be, remember that.'

But Dad was wrong. There's only a moment in any life when everything is possible, and that moment is finite. Things happen, no way back.

So now I say nothing.

Dad doesn't seem to notice. 'And I let Aidan down, too. If I hadn't encouraged his interest in the bike, he might never have been tempted to take off on it.' He shakes his head, brushes a hand across his face, 'Guess I was arrogant enough to think I could give him something he didn't have at home.'

'He told me to tell you he was sorry, Dad.'

His head jerks up, 'For what?'

'Taking the bike …'

I catch the glint of tears before he turns away, lifts the coffee pot off the stove.

'Something you might not know, Shaun. Not long after Aidan died, Jack put Maura in hospital. She nearly died.' He stops, rakes a hand through his hair, 'Lord knows what that family endured over the years. Anyway, he's in jail, won't be getting out any time soon.'

There's the sound of a motor cutting off outside, the slam of a car door. Seconds later, Mom arrives, a navy hospital apron covering most of her bright blue top and dark skirt. Thinner, a little hunched. New, deeper lines carved into her forehead.

Dad pours himself a mug of coffee, drops a kiss on the top of her head, then goes to the door, 'Talk later, Shaun.'

I nod, avoid his eyes.

Mom says, 'Ed was on the phone earlier. He's looking to talk to you.'

She's wasting her breath this time. If Ed doesn't get how uncool it is to be with Ella's sister, there's nothing to say.

I turn back to the window. 'Do me a favour, Mom, next time he rings, tell him I've gone out.'

Her eyes cloud. She picks up dirty dishes from the table, brings them to where I'm leaning against the sink, says softly,

'Don't you think it's time, Shaun? You need to allow yourself to forget. And this thing with Ed and Sarah, they're just living their lives, nothing to do with you. You can't put off talking to him forever.'

'Not sure you're right about that, Mom.'

Yesterday was enough to show me that my folks are moving on and I don't need Mom telling me what I already know. That I'm the one left behind.

Her shoulders tense and I'm immediately sorry. 'Look, I have stuff to do but I'll talk to him before I leave.' I'm putting her off, and she knows it, but it's the best I can dredge up right now. 'Promise.'

She nods, hesitates, 'You and I haven't talked properly either, Shaun.'

Here it comes, the moment I knew had to happen. Last night, we were careful, grazed the perimeters with superficial chat but Mom was never going to leave it. She thinks she let me down, doesn't get that me taking off to London wasn't about her, or Dad.

I shove over to give her space to dump the dishes in the sink, then she turns back to me. Waits.

'We've talked on the phone,' I remind her, gripping the back of a kitchen chair, feel the soft give of my denim jacket, hanging there since last night. 'I'm sorry for leaving without telling you, but Irene phoned as soon as I arrived, so you knew I was with her …' I tail off.

'Yes, but talking on the phone is never the same as face to face.'

'Look, Mom, I couldn't handle staying here, being so close to … everything,' I say, straightening up, pushing the chair in tight under the table. Random images jumping like a broken movie reel inside my head. Shoving jeans and tee-shirts into my rucksack, bank notes from my Saturday job into my back pocket. Head pounding as the sick truth swept through me, over and over: it was down to me that Aidan was dead and there was nothing I could do to bring him back.

He was gone. Forever. The only thing I could do was not be here either.

When I look up, Mom is on the verge of tears.

'Mom, please don't tell me it wasn't my fault, I don't need to hear it.'

'We don't see what happened the way you do, Shaun. No-one does,' taking a tissue from her pocket, wiping her eyes.

I want to say, that's because you don't know what I know. But I don't. What Dad has just told me about Aidan, about Jack, makes some sense of how he was with me. Makes everything worse.

'Mike, the owner of the café is retiring, he wants me to take over the lease.' My voice light, anything to break the tension, change the subject. I've been managing the café for more than a year now. The money isn't great, it's never gonna be my dream job, but no-one knows me there, or what happened. It's given me space and between breaths, I've had the idea I might like to write, but I'm not sure. Not yet.

'You can do anything you like, love, you always could,' Mom says with a less watery smile.

'You and Dad should come over to visit,' the invitation out before I can think about it. 'Not that I'll be able to put you up, I only have one room,' I add quickly, 'But we can organise something … Kathy will probably have a suggestion on places to stay …' I tail off, already seeing the gleam in Mom's eyes.

'Kathy? I haven't heard you mention her before?'

'Don't get any ideas, Mom. Kathy is someone who comes

in a few days a week to help with service and some of the food.' Not mentioning that recently I'm getting the vibe Kathy might like more from our friendship than I'm willing to give. 'Anyway, forget London. Let's just enjoy these few days, please, Mom? I'm over what happened, everything is fine.'

The phone rings, she tenses.

I swallow the last of my coffee, reach for Dad's windcheater hanging from a peg on the door, 'Gonna take a quick walk. Back in a while.'

I slip-slide through the remains of a light fall of snow, head towards the beach. The garden is winter sad, yellowed plants, odd clumps of woody lavender, spiky dead heads, smell of wet soil and Dad's jacket leaching Old Spice and tobacco.

There's a screech above my head, a lone seagull hovers in the crease of a breeze, then paints an arc, merges in the grey blue sky. Darker clouds shade the horizon, threaten rain. Snow rarely settles here, too close to the beach, a huge disappointment for me and Ed when we were kids.

Without thinking, I vault the rusted iron gate, still half-off its hinges, land on the beach the far side. A muscle memory that brings a smile.

My runners sink in the sand, leave a trail of footsteps. I'm the only one on the beach, no boys trying out smokes in the dunes, no lovers sharing a first kiss. No dog walkers, no headcases taking a swim in the freezing Atlantic waters. Just my shadow in the mist, the roar of waves, the shriek of a lonely seagull.

I turn off the beach, runners squelching, across a reed-filled, marshy field, in the direction of town a few miles away.

No-one sees what happened the way you do.

Mom and Dad will never understand, not while they don't know the truth.

The truth, a scab I can't help picking. A compulsion to take it out, examine it, analyse it, imagine how differently things might have turned out if only…

… and then, when I've revisited that New Year's Eve three years ago, everything I could have done differently, all the ways it was my fault, I put the truth back, until the next time.

The folks were going to some of Mom's family for a party, planned to be away for the night. A free pass to organise some festivities of my own, just a select few, some friends from school and, of course, Ella.

They flapped about whether to go, worried about the forecast of extreme weather, the state of the roads. Had me on edge most of the day wondering if I'd have to cancel. Everything woulda been different if only the storm had set in earlier, if they hadn't travelled.

But it didn't and they did, even though lightning was slicing the sky when they decided to chance it, a miserable and complaining Ed in the back seat of the Dyane. Sulking because Dad insisted he go with them, 'You're too young, Ed. Next year, you can make your own choice, but for now, you're with us. Try to make the most of it.'

Yeah, now I can imagine how Ed felt, but back then, I was so wrapped up in my own head, mostly thinking about having Ella to myself at Monksfield, his disappointment hardly registered. I guess he coulda squealed on me, told the folks about my party, but to be fair, he didn't. Another if only.

Once the tail-lights of Dad's car disappeared down the

lane, I flicked on every light in the house, put some Bowie on the turntable, switched up the volume, grabbed a can of beer. Not long after, friends began arriving with plastic bags bulging with booze.

Everyone, except Ella.

The plan was she'd tell her parents she was spending the night with a friend from school and then, once she'd managed to leave the house, phone for a hackney cab from the box at the end of Main Street. Neither of us factored in the weather.

When she hadn't arrived by ten o'clock, I was already wondering what to do. If I called her at home, one of her parents was likely to answer and if it was her notoriously strict Dad, I'd be causing problems for Ella. But if I didn't make the call, I wouldn't know what was happening. Why she wasn't here.

By the time I did pick up the phone, the line had been knocked out by the storm.

Disappointment drilled a hole in my gut. No point dressing it up, I was feeling pretty sorry for myself. And then, maybe it was the drink I'd already had, but my brain went into overdrive and I convinced myself that rather than being prevented from leaving home, she'd never intended to come at all. She was ditching me. We were over.

By then, I'd liberated some whiskey from the drinks' cabinet and alone in my bedroom, with the party rocking downstairs, that last, stupid idea gained traction. Made me frantic to know for sure.

I needed to find Ella, talk to her.

The house lights were out, as well as the phone, the music on the record player replaced by someone strumming guitar. The girls had located candles and the soft glow made the house and everyone in it ethereal. My head was all over the place, any possibility was a potential reality, any reality no more than vague possibility. Some of the lads were draped on the stairs, smoking, drinking, shouting over each other. A few messers tried to grab me as I staggered towards the kitchen, but I shook them off, grabbed a key off the hook beside the back door.

The wind was howling, rain sheeting down and I was drenched through before I'd gone more than a few steps, not that I remember getting wet, or going into the garage. Didn't even notice the light coming through the window, until I threw open the door. Then the musty smell of paraffin hit me and I realised the lamp Dad kept on a shelf for emergencies had been lit.

Aidan was half-sitting, half-lying, against the bare block wall, watching me out of red rimmed, bruised eyes as I stood, swaying, light-headed, trying to make sense of him being there, the blood congealing around his nose, the swollen, cut lips.

'Were you in a fight? You look like you were in a fight …' I was rambling, stupid with drink and the shock of finding him.

'Same as always, Shaunie, can never see what's under your nose.' His voice a mumble.

I must have looked as confused as I felt because then he muttered, 'Yes, Shaunie, I've been in a fight … I mean, that's what I do, isn't it?'

He looked away, and then, with a groan, hauled himself up. I edged away, an instinctive recoil down to those times when he was the one doling out the pain and I was on the receiving end.

As I took in the damage to his face, the careful way he was holding himself, I can't remember any stir of pity. I'd loathed Aidan too long by then, not just because of the humiliations he'd inflicted, but also his closeness to Dad. If I'd known the whole story, if I'd known then about Jack, would I have behaved differently? I'm not gonna lie, probably not. And like I said before, things move on, there's no way back.

That night, Aidan was what he always had been to me, an unwanted intrusion and more than that, a hindrance to my half-baked plan to take the bike into town to find Ella.

'What are you doing out here anyway? Go back to your fucking party,' he grunted, leaning against the wall to stay upright.

I flashed the key and when he saw it, his expression changed. 'You haven't a clue how to handle the bike, don't even think about it.'

But I was ahead of him. 'I may not have to, now you're here.'

There was a short silence and he read something in my face, because he grunted, 'No way … you think I'll take the bike out for you? Not a fucking chance.'

'You will, Aidan, here's why …' and even in my own ears, my voice didn't sound like mine.

There's a screech above my head. The seagull has trailed me to the graveyard.

I have no idea how to locate the grave, there's no list posted anywhere either inside or outside the walls, or at the gate, so I walk from the end of each row of headstones to the next, scanning names. Aidan's is close to the overhanging branches of a yew tree at the back. A plain grey stone, the edges around the plot more of the same. His name picked out in white:

Aidan Stephen Doyle
28th April 1957 – 1st January 1976.

The words don't look familiar, the name could belong to anyone. I'm standing at the side of a sodden plot on a sodden day, waiting for a ghost.

There's a cough and I twist round, find a fair-haired, square set man close by, maybe late twenties, not much older than me. Watching from beneath heavy, hooded eyes, dark brows. A hint of day-old stubble on his chin, fists stuffed into the pockets of a black coat he looks sewn into, white clerical collar just visible above a grey wool scarf.

'It's Shaun, isn't it?'

'Yes, Father,' schooldays respect another muscle memory, too many in the ether today. His face looks familiar.

'Thought so,' he nods, almost absentmindedly. 'I'm Tarran Hyland, we haven't met, but I know your parents, and Ed, of course. He's like you.'

'I've seen your photo in school, Father. You were on the team that brought back the Cup.'

'Call me Tarran,' brushing aside the formality as he aims a leather booted foot at pebbles on the path, 'School seems like another life.'

His coat ripples as he moves, still in good shape.

'Everyone thought you were headed for Connaught.'

'So did I, for a while, but God had other plans,' with a glance down at his black garb and a grin, 'What you might call a fork in the road.'

I nod, know what he means. 'So, how do you know Ed? Did you teach in St Muireadeach's?' referring to our local college.

'Yes, a few terms after leaving the seminary, getting my H.Dip. I've been away since, in Africa … ' he breaks off as if reluctant to say more. Then he looks at me, 'What about you?'

Maybe it's the mention of school, of Ed, but as our eyes meet, something opens up between us, as if we've met before, already know each other.

'I've been in London for the last few years,' I mutter reluctantly, aiming one of my runners in the same direction of the pebbles, 'just home for a few days.'

Digging his hands into his pockets again, I get the feeling he's on the point of moving off, but instead, he nods towards a black granite stone a few rows away, 'Just paying my mother a last visit before heading off.'

'Back to Africa?'

'No, Glasgow of all places. The Bishop has decided that's where I'm needed most,' an unmistakeable curl on his lips.

There not much I can think of to say to that, but to be fair, it's my first and only deep and meaningful with a priest in a graveyard.

As if shaking off his own thoughts, he gestures towards Aidan's grave, 'This lad was your cousin? I remember Ed telling me he could be a bit of a hard case?'

'I suppose he was, in a way,' I say slowly, wondering about Ed. How much he knew, how much he'd seen.

'Sad thing to happen,' laying his hand on the stone briefly in silent communication.

'This is the first time I've been here.'

'And is it helping?' His voice sharp as a scalpel, keen eyes on my face again, leaving no space for anything but truth.

I shrug, 'I'm not the one who died.'

No idea where that comes from, but then it's as if the

words inside my head will explode, that I'll explode, if I don't tell this man everything.

'Aidan thought I was going to tell my Dad about stuff, things he'd done … unless he did what I wanted, that's why he took the bike … ' I brush a hand across my face, my fingers come away wet.

Tarran Hyland just says, 'I see,' but when I glance at him, the look on his face makes me race on, words tripping over themselves.

'I wanted him to give me a lift into town to find Ella … she was my girlfriend … but he didn't wait for me, took off on his own. Everyone thinks he stole the bike, was drunk …,' I stop, but need to finish now I've started. 'None of that's true. Aidan was in a bad place, and instead of trying to help, I made it worse.'

I glance up, meet the priest's eyes, 'So, yeah, it's my fault he's dead.'

He says nothing, but I have the sense he gets what I'm saying. As soon as I made the threat, it felt wrong. I felt wrong. Aidan had slumped back against the wall, any fight left in him, draining away. Then, with a twisted grin, he shook his head slowly, 'Your Dad has been good to me, Shaunie, but I always knew he'd find out I wasn't worth the effort.'

He gestured for the key and I lobbed it to him. From the way he was moving, slowly, awkwardly, I could see he was hurting, but he managed to drag himself onto the bike.

When he growled, 'Open the door,' I yanked it wide open, then ran back to climb on behind him. But he had already powered up the bike, shouted as he roared past, 'Tell Uncle John I'm sorry.'

No-one knows what happened then. Whether it was the wind, the rain, if Aidan was going too fast. If it was something else. Whatever, the bike went into a slide on a corner just outside the town.

Tarran Hyland is watching me, hasn't taken his eyes off my face, soaking up the truth as if he's been travelling with me, with Aidan, in my head.

I rub tears from my face, the first I've shed. For Aidan and yeah, for myself. Meet the priest's eyes, 'I owe it to Aidan to tell the truth but I can't do it in a way that sounds as if I'm making excuses for myself or wrecks Dad's memory of him.'

He shrugs deeper into his coat, 'I'd say your Dad probably had a sound enough reading on Aidan, so what you tell him might not come as much of a surprise. Grief has a way of painting the world its own shade. We all do things we regret but the great thing is having the chance … and maybe the need … to do better.'

Plops of rain, loud in the quiet between us, begin to stain the grey stone on Aidan's grave.

The priest straightens up, 'Well, I suppose I should be getting on, Shaun. Remember me to your parents and to Ed.'

With a vague sketch of a blessing, he strides away, towards the gate, leaving me alone.

A breeze shivers through the bare branches of the yew tree. The gull lands a few feet away, swats at an old ice cream wrapper. Ignores me.

Ignores the ghosts.

It's later that evening. The lights of the pub shimmer through a mist-filled rain, the Christmas decorations still in place, a massive tree in the square blinks coloured lights. Santa grins frantically from his sleigh, perched above the door. I wait for a moment, listening to the throb of music, steady myself to meet people I haven't met in a while.

As I push open the door, the din is enveloping. Try to hide a smile. My moron of a brother is at the bar, money in hand, wearing my denim jacket again.

No sign of Sarah. Or Ella. Not that I'm expecting her to be here. Too much has happened, too much silence. Something else that's down to me. She phoned our house the morning Aidan died. I wouldn't talk to her, left that to Mom. Ella told her she hadn't been allowed out because of the storm, one good decision in a sea of bad ones.

I guess my self-loathing back then extended to Ella too and in a twisted, irrational way, I blamed her for some of what happened. If only she'd turned up for the party, if only she'd phoned before the line went dead, I wouldn't have drunk too much, wouldn't have taken the key for the bike, wouldn't have found Aidan in the garage, and on and on into infinity. More 'if only's.'

Which all sounds pathetic now.

The folks are dancing, a two-piece band doing their best with Dad's favourite, Dean Martin. They look happy, Mom giggling. She sees me, waves and Dad raises his eyebrows, makes a face. Pretends he's not into this as much as she is.

There are things that need to be said, but talking can wait for tomorrow. I thought everything since Aidan's death was about guilt, it never occurred to me there could be grief there, too. For a boy with hopes and dreams, a boy who could have been my best friend. Most of all, the boy Dad believed in.

Something else I've finally figured out: not all the shit things that happen need to be shared. I'll tell the folks enough to make sense of the night Aidan died, enough to help them understand, the rest can stay between me and him, between cousins. The way it should be.

Ed comes over, 'Hey, bro, there's someone here who wants to see you,' nodding towards the end of the bar. Sarah is there, on a high stool. When she sees me, she nudges another girl sitting with her back to me.

The girl glances around. Our eyes catch. Ella.

3: 1989

NINA

By the time they navigate the mist-greyed outskirts of Ballinasloe, pull up outside Hayden's Hotel in the yellow Ford Escort, Nina has a stitch in her side with stress. Miss Lambert yanks hard on the handbrake, looks at her.

'We should eat,' she says.

Her face has the worried set Nina is used to now, but her large brown eyes are soft. Kind. Nina nods. Tries to indicate agreement, emits a guttural noise. A strangled sound. They've barely spoken since they left Dublin, and she doesn't trust herself to words. Best to shore her voice up in case it comes out small, weak. Worse. Pleading.

Nina is wearing ratty Converse and forest green tights, her school duffel coat over a summer skirt of her mother's which cuts mid-skinny-calf – a print of peonies, faded – Natascha's Dunnes sweatshirt, a fashionable shade of grey, which she has loaned grudgingly. The O'Neill's holdall in the boot is crammed with similar donations. Natascha, four years older, bigger boned, resents her, generally, but more now, and

Nina wonders again at her sister's ability to make all crises somehow about herself. Their mother had suggested she bring her school uniform. The skirts they bought in Arnotts in first year with 'room for growth' are still big on her with expanders. But Miss Lambert said that probably wouldn't be appropriate. It's only for a short time, and, well, she was sure Father Hyland would be able to point them in the right direction for anything she might need.

They walk side by side through the foyer, past a neatly pressed brunette at the reception desk, a stairway rising majestically to the left, garlanded and fairylit, a Christmas tree winking in a sea of red and gold carpet inviting them through double doors. Nina feels a clutch in her chest, as if her lungs have violently contracted. Airless, she says:
  'Will I be able to go home for Christmas?'
  Miss Lambert shakes her head.
  'I don't think so, pet'.

Miss Lambert queues for soup and sandwiches while Nina sits at one of the dark wood tables, small and busy, a butt-filled ashtray and newly laid beermats. It's gone half past twelve and customers with the confident gait of regulars are filing in slowly.
  A woman, white-haired, wizened in a tweed skirt and a pale pink jumper is navigating a Zimmer frame to a pre-set destination, trailed by a melancholic looking middle-aged man. She falters, looks blearily at Nina for a moment, before the man helps her move on. Nina pulls the duffel coat tighter, a wave of guilt rushing through her, a ridiculous urge to run

to the woman, to excuse herself, explain she is not mitching school.

In a recess, two heavy-set men in suits sit kinglike, preparing to feast on plates heaped with roast beef, limp runner beans, mashed and roasted potatoes, lurking beneath a fast-setting skin of gravy. Pints of Guinness. One of them winks at her. She looks away.

A lounge boy, no older than herself, in an ill-fitting shirt, approaches as if to ask for her order, catches her eye for a second. Hesitates. Looks away.

She turns her focus to one of the beermats, pinches it between her thumb and forefinger, turns it intently, the cardboard compelling as silk under her fingertips. A waft of hops and cooked food catches her by surprise. A memory of a drink-hazed morning. A small rush to gag, which she chokes back in practiced response. The baby in her belly kicks. She pushes her hand in hard to hush it.

Now her secret is known to a few, it has somehow made it more shameful. An image on repeat in her head: lying on the bed in Dr Kavanagh's surgery, her mother upright and rigid in the consulting chair, as if this were her own medical issue. The man's fat yellow-stained fingers poking repeatedly at the hinted mound of her stomach, digging deep.

'She's quite far advanced,' he'd said.

And maybe she'd imagined the emphasis on the word advanced, but she doesn't think so. Advanced – beyond where she should be. The opposite of innocent. An outlier, outsider. A boundary broken. Smashed.

'When? How?' her mother had said, her face quite colourless.

'I'm afraid this bird has flown some time ago. I'd say she's almost six months gone,' the man said.

Miss Lambert arrives with a tray, moves the ashtray aside. Arranges the soup – tomato – and toasted sandwiches – ham and cheese – two glasses of water, between them. Wipes a stray streak of congealed mayonnaise gifted from a previous customer with a burgundy coloured napkin. Nina is starving. But. She doesn't like tomato soup. Hates, in fact, tomato soup. The look, the texture, are enough to tip tears from her lids. The smell tickles a volcano of hunger in her stomach. Something else. Her hatred of tomatoes is known. A running joke. A discussion about food they disliked in class one day. Nina told a long, involved story about her mother's soup diet, a misused bottle of ketchup, a performance Nina didn't know she had in her. She'd scrunched her face up at the end and Miss Lambert had laughed. They all had. A wave of energy which lit her. A happy slagging from her peers, even from Miss Lambert herself. Inclusion. 'Don't mention tomatoes to Nina, she doesn't even like the colour red!'

She sits on her hands, a rough patch in the velour, a cigarette burn. Maybe it's all they have on the menu today. Maybe Miss Lambert has simply forgotten. After all, the woman teaches hundreds of girls.

Nina picks at the sandwich. Eyes the soup. Eyes her teacher. Tries to imagine how there was ever any sort of humour or ease between them, is sure there was, wonders if it is only confounded now by The Situation. Each of them sifting any twitch or shift, any small talk, for potential relevance to The

Situation, The Situation underlying and undermining any talk at all. The need to keep boundaries clear. Miss Lambert is her designated protector for the duration. She is not her saviour. Nina needs to remember this. She, Nina, is beyond redemption.

'Will I be able to go back to school?' she says. 'Afterwards?'

Miss Lambert hesitates, chews on her sandwich. Washes it down with a swig of water. Lowers the glass from lipstickless lips.

'I guess it depends,' she says. 'You might be able to repeat sixth year. Start again in September. You would have been young doing your leaving cert anyway, wouldn't you? When's your birthday?'

Nina takes a drink of water.

'First of November,' she says.

'You'd still be eighteen doing the exams.'

'Will I be able to go back to St Eithne's?'

Miss Lambert's face curls in a stuck, distanced sympathy, a small shake of her head, which sends a wave of panic through the girl.

'I don't know, Nina.'

'The house is called Monksfield,' Miss Lambert says, 'Monksfield House. It's right on the sea, by a beach, you'll be able to go for walks. When it's quiet.'

Nina says nothing. They're back in the car, eyes straight ahead, Miss Lambert's chatter more awkward than the silence before. She imagines herself walking along a deserted beach at dusk, her belly, which is still neat, growing larger and rounder, her shame distended and displayed, heralding her approach like a bell.

'Father Hyland is an old family friend,' Miss Lambert says. 'I've known him since I was little. A bit of a rugby hero, before he joined the seminary. Taught in St Muireadeach's. You'll like him.'

'Will there be other girls there?'

'I don't know, Nina. It depends. The Church bought the house off a family in the area a few years ago. I don't think they've had girls like you there yet.'

'Girls like me?'

And Miss Lambert, hands rigid at ten to two, shrugs stiffly.

'You know what I mean.'

Nina does. Nina knows she is lucky. Knows this peculiar and particular arrangement is because her parents have standing in the community, an in with the nuns. Old money, the perception of it, the power of it, if not the actuality of it. Knows this is a special arrangement, and if she were another 'girl like her', she would be put straight into Temple Hill or the like. Knows also this is to protect her father, a High Court judge, from scandal.

If her pregnancy hadn't been so advanced, she would have ended up like Laura Doyle, on a boat to England with her mother, the issue never spoken of again. Her wiggling squiggling companion gone. When she thinks thoughts like these, she rubs her belly. Stifles tears. The confusion of emotions too much for her small frame.

The house is detached, incongruous, like something from Hammer House of Horror re-runs, the original Victorian façade thrown into chaos with windows butchered to let in more light. A porch area, complete with beat-up wicker furniture. The beach opposite is long and stone strewn, small strips of sand, more Lough Derg than Majorca.

'The previous owner was an American,' Father Hyland says, as if by way of explanation or apology, Miss Lambert trailing him with a small overnight case Nina covets. Powder blue with cream stitching, chrome handle and locks. Nina follows, awkwardly dangling her holdall.

The priest is above average tall, and handsome, Nina thinks, in an older man sort of way. Neat cut fair hair tickling the edge of his pure white collar. As if activated by his presence, Miss Lambert is changed: eyes bright, touching her hair, smiling. Vivacious. Beautiful. Nina's stomach does a flip, unease rising in her like a glob of wax in a lava lamp. Red.

'I'll show you to your rooms,' he says. 'Or would you prefer tea first? No, maybe rooms first, then I'll make some tea. You must be hungry. And tired.'

The man seems flustered. Miss Lambert has this effect on men. Nina has seen it before. On the trip to Cork in April, the International Choral Festival. The way they become alert when she enters the room. The way the air seems to tingle. Nina's head time shuffles. The astonishing thought that they are here, in this awkward exchange, because of that trip. An image, blurred and confused, lips, hands, vomit, intrudes on her thoughts. She pushes it away.

Nina is the youngest in her family. Ivan, Natascha, Alexander and herself, boy, girl, boy, girl, all two years apart. A houseful of loud liberal ideas and ideals underpinned with, it turns out, a healthy foundation of Catholic conservatism.

This house has a creak and a feel to it Nina is familiar with. High ceilings, cornicing, large fireplaces. Cracked plaster, exposed brick, sloping floors. An air of damp and rot which would excite her mother, launch her into an interrogation of Father Hyland about its history. Plans for its restoration. A long diatribe about preservation of original features.

Nina can almost see her face, startling blue eyes high with excitement, a passion for physical inanimate things, a face at odds with the blank canvas she has worn when dealing with the logistics involved in her daughter's predicament. She wonders when they will see each other again, thinks it won't bother her if it is a long time.

She is shown to a room at the back of the house, bright with windows on right-angled walls. Somebody has whitewashed the uneven surfaces and there's a rag rug on the floor, a rainbow striped duvet set. The window frames are painted green, an unexpected low beam of sunlight giving the space a holiday vibe at odds with the darkening December day. She drops her holdall on the floor, sits on the bed, bounces on it to test the firmness of the mattress. Feels light in the moment. As if she might, in fact, be here on a holiday. A normal sixteen year old, doing normal sixteen year old things. She notices the stand in the corner, an old-fashioned bowl and jug for washing and over it, not a mirror, but a crucifix. A familiar dread. Shades of Rosemary's Baby, a vision of the room transformed, her body confined to the bed, racked in agony, a woman, a nun, maybe, standing guard, grim and scornful.

She unpacks and makes her way down the rickety stairs, unsure of where she is going, her desire to escape, for flight, moving her arms and legs independently.

'There you are,' Miss Lambert says, as she reaches the end with a half-trip. 'Father Tarran has tea ready for us.'

Nina nods and follows to the kitchen to sit at a table with a cream and orange oilcloth offering white bread ham sandwiches and a sweaty Swiss Roll. She accepts tea brewed to black in a brown and cream striped cup, the saucer chipped, a bare drop of milk. Her mother would call it an apology. But at least if she is drinking tea, eating, she has something to do with her hands, her mouth. Seconds of relief, concentrated effort, where what is expected of her is clear.

'Lisa tells me you're a great singer,' the priest says.

Lisa.

His eyes are over-eager, over-friendly. Somehow vulnerable, as if he is struggling to make all this right too. Normal. And Nina wants to put him at ease, for him, for them all, to be at ease, for her not to be the centre of attention, but she is unsure how to answer. She can hardly say 'Yes, I have a beautiful voice,' because this is vanity, behaviour her mother would describe as 'being forward', and yet she can hardly deny she sings well when her music teacher is here, sitting at the table, entitled, maybe, to some share of the praise.

'Miss Lambert is a great teacher,' she says, finally, feeling like she has invaded the staff room, been called to account for gross misdoing.

'There's no need to be modest, Nina, you've a beautiful voice,' Miss Lambert – Lisa – says, smiling at Father Tarran.

'We've a great choir in St Muireadeach's. We're hoping to go to Cork next year.'

'Oh, we were in Cork this year, weren't we, Nina? Our choir made the semi-finals.'

'Well, we're always open to new members.'

'Oh, I've only an average voice, compared to Nina.'

And this is the conversation killer. A segue to an invitation for Nina, which all three know won't be issued. Nina is here in this strange world for a specific time, a specific purpose. She has no friends, does not know anybody, apart from Miss Lambert, who is going home. Nina wants to go home. She can't picture that either. She and her stomach are creatures of the underworld, the shadows. Here, but not here. A problem to be managed. Less than that. A ghost. Not solid enough to be displayed even as a cautionary tale.

There are five for breakfast next morning. Nina, Miss Lambert, Father Hyland and two others introduced, without further detail, as Mark and Siobhán. They sit in the formal dining room, a long table with mismatched linen and cheap white crockery, while a middle-aged woman, introduced as Mrs Kelly, brings plates weary with sausages and bacon and eggs. Fried tomatoes spill their guts towards their companions, making Nina feel sick. She pushes the food around the plate. Aware of the eyes on her. On her stomach, which seems to have grown.

Siobhán looks to be in her mid-twenties. Tallish, bony, a wispy sort of pretty. Nina glances at her stomach, but it is flat. Nina smiles, the girl returns it and Nina is touched by the sadness in this smile, a depth of weariness stretching across the table. Palpable.

Mark is younger, maybe even younger than Nina, dark west of Ireland handsome, something odd in the movement of him, something slightly off. He grins at her, but not in the leering way other boys do, more a partner-in-crime recognition. As if to say, shucks, here we are now, both caught red-handed. Ah well.

'We're a bit of a mish mash, Nina,' Father Tarran says. 'I'm not sure what Lisa has told you about Monksfield?'

'Not much, Tarran. I know very little myself,' Miss Lambert says.

She looks so pretty this morning, Nina thinks. Casual, young, jeans and a Breton jumper, blue suede ankle boots. Her dark hair falling neat on her shoulders, washed. Her eyes are alive, clear with freedom. Nina wants to shout at her. Wants to shake her. Shock her into a different reality, but what this reality looks like, Nina has no clue. She feels this often, as if she is living in a parallel universe, or a comic book, her real life obscured by a thin veil, almost accessible. If she could step into it, un-take some misstep, a step which has something and nothing to do with the baby, everything might go back to normal.

'Well, we're still trying to figure it out ourselves. The church bought the house with a donation from a benefactor, a man from the area. He gave money on the premise that it would be used to set up a facility for young people in need. The definition of 'need' was loose, but we're interpreting it as a kind of halfway house project, a respite, somewhere people get a second chance.'

As he talks, Nina feels in him what her mother would call 'presence', charisma, can see him give this speech in a town hall, at a fundraiser, and can see that, in the moment of saying it, he believes every word. He has an honest look. A twitch of her dad, who can convince himself of any argument so passionately he can convince the world. Then turn around and argue the opposite point equally. Nina will give the baby up for adoption. Nina will keep the baby. Nina should not be pregnant in the first place. As if it were an intellectual conundrum.

'You three are our first guests,' Father Tarran says. 'Siobhán has been with us a couple of months, has been a great help to us, to me, in defining our vision. Mark is here only a few days before you, Nina.'

Mark grins at her.

'You're all welcome to share your personal stories with each other, or not,' the priest continues. 'There's no pressure. I'm always here if you simply want to talk. And of course, we provide food and lodgings and medical attention as required.'

He seems to avoid looking at Nina when he says this, and it sparks a panic in her which she tries to quell. An ask which is becoming familiar to her, words she can't form into a coherent question. She feels impossibly visible: round, shining, huge. An obvious and pressing problem. How will, who will, she ask for this help when she needs it? This man? Siobhán? Mark? Will they run with hot water and towels, hold her hand through contractions? She longs for the presence of those nightmare nuns. Their sure-handed competence, even if it is dealt with large helpings of shame and blame.

'In return,' he continues, a spot of grease on the newly painted wall behind him catching and holding Nina's eye, anchoring her. 'We ask only that you help out with some jobs around the house, some of the renovations. We've been painting and getting the rooms ready for more guests. How do you like yours?'

She manages a small nod.

'It's lovely.'

'Right, well,' Father Hyland says. 'I think we're all going to get along just splendidly.'

'I'm sure you will,' Miss Lambert says, rising.

Nina feels a chill. The cord to life as she knows it, about to be cut. After everything, a sticky-sweet smile will be their final sign off. She is cargo, has been delivered, checked in, and in the symbolic act of Miss Lambert standing, she, Nina, is somebody else's problem.

'Are you going?'
A distinct relief in the woman's shrug.
'I'm afraid I have to, Nina.'

The yellow Ford Escort pulls out of the driveway, the glug of the choke firing the engine echoes in Nina's stomach, nausea vying for space with the baby. She thinks she might vomit, wants to cry. Instead, she closes her eyes, breathes, in, deep, out, slow release. A meditation technique she learned on a school retreat, grounds herself in the room. There is bustle. Siobhán and Mark are clearing away the breakfast delft and Mrs Kelly clears her throat in a pointed manner, gives her a sly look as she directs all three to wash, dry, points to the relevant repositories for clean ware.

'I'm here to do for Father Tarran, ye three can look after yerselves,' she says.

Nina takes the hint and busies herself transporting dish plates.

'When are you due? 'Siobhán says, her eyes lifting, Princess Dianaesque, from the sink.

'February, I think.'

Mark hands her a bowl to stow away.

'You were ridin',' he says, with a grin.

After breakfast Father Tarran tells them they are free until 10.30am. He is planning another painting project, another bedroom to the back of the house, but he needs to go buy more paint. He brings Mark with him and Siobhán disappears too, without saying anything. Nina doesn't know what to do, where to be, so she goes back to her room.

She settles to read but she has brought only a few books, one of which is Wuthering Heights, from her English curriculum. She'd wanted to bring all her books. Wanted to push through and do her Christmas exams. The summer exams. Continue as if missing months of school is normal. Her mother argued against it. Said that she wouldn't be in any state to traipse into St Eithne's almost right after giving birth. She has no idea of how life-altering, life-ending the experience will be. This is how it goes between them now. Little prods of fear which do no good except perhaps to scratch at her mother's anger, bring her some kind of temporary relief. And Nina, in a fit of defiance, asked her where did she think the neighbours would think she was? Her golf club buddies? Did she really think they would buy 'gone to mind granny' in Leaving Cert year? But. Nina is learning that truth is secondary to a story which might in any way be considered plausible. Nobody has addressed the big question, which is only her question, undisclosed, undiscussed, undreamt of by the adults: what if she wants to keep the baby?

She smooths the duvet, the fresh cover, not washed or ironed yet. Creased with new. A polyester mix, a strange feeling to Nina. All bed linen at home is 'good', has been handed through the ages, starched and ironed by various housekeepers. Crisp, uncomfortable, cold. Worn in patches. She liked the way this duvet folded into her last night, wrapped itself around her stomach, like a hug. Despite the windows, despite the age of the house, it seems the Church – or the former American resident – has installed central heating and the room temperature is snug. She'd slept, a deep dreamless sleep. All energy spent.

Before they start painting, they have tea and Fig Rolls, presented on a tray by Mrs Kelly, with a large dose of grump. Siobhán is back, changed into paint spattered jeans and a tee shirt. Nina can see now that she is wiry rather than skinny, with defined triceps. Strong. Mark and Father Tarran are similarly kitted in old cords and jeans and jumpers.

'I don't have any painting clothes,' Nina says.

Father Tarran looks at her.

'Give me a second.'

He disappears. Nina has a vision of him reappearing with a cassock or a habit. Her, hunkered under a wimple, delicately painting skirting boards thick with masking tape. But he arrives back with already spattered man jeans, an AC/DC tee shirt and a smile.

'We'll put you on wall duty,' he says. 'So's you don't have to bend.'

Such small kindness is so unexpected, Nina finds she can't answer him. Nods.

Siobhán notices, smiles at her.

Nina changes, commandeers a workworn roller, folds yellow paint into a black tray. Covers the roller to an adequate consistency. Nina is used to DIY. Her parents' house is an ever unfurling project.

She settles into the rhythm of the work, radio Nova playing a medley of hits, Mark singing tunefully along. A passable Freddie Mercury impersonation – I want to break free – which she and Siobhán crack up at, the atmosphere sunny, the baby squiggling happily. Every time this happens she's surprised she's not horrified, that it doesn't feel like an alien invasion. Instead, she is overcome with a desire to protect. To see, to check her baby. To count fingers and toes and make an inventory of all other equipment required. To fill this child with love.

'Does the daddy know?' Siobhán says.

Nina doesn't know how to answer this. If she tells the truth, Siobhán might think her a slut. If she tells one lie, she might tie herself into a web of lies.

'Who is it, Nina? You have to tell us. Is it that Tom Macken fella?'

Her mother had badgered her. An image of her dragging Nina up to Tom Macken's mother's doorstep, the thought of Tom Macken, with his supercilious little grin even knowing she was pregnant, that she'd had sex with a boy, horrified her.

'It has nothing to do with Tom Macken,' she'd said.

'You mean you don't want him to know? He has a right to know, Nina.'

'I mean, he's not the father.'

'Then who is the father?'

'I don't know.'

'What do you mean you don't know? Dear Jesus, is there more than one option? Have you been opening your legs for the entire male population of South County Dublin?'

'Stop it! Stop it! Stop it!'

'You should have been saying that six months ago.'

So Nina stopped saying anything at all. Pretty much. When the baby stopped moving for three days, she didn't mention it. To anybody. She poked and prodded and tried to imagine how she would feel if her baby was dead. And what she felt, she was sure, was grief. All twists and inconsistencies and shades of it. Her prayers from the early days of knowing answered, her problem solved. Everybody could move on. But. They couldn't. She couldn't.

Now the fact of it was out, now her parents, her brothers, assumed her guilt as their own, as if it was their responsibility to protect her, their responsibility she had fallen pregnant, their responsibility she will forever be considered a liability. Regardless. And when the baby started moving again, there was nobody to share her relief. Her secret joy. There was only her mother, organising things, talking to the school, talking to the priest. Her father's quiet disapproval. Sister Anselm's stern disappointment. Miss Lambert's disbelief.

Her teacher must have known, must have worked out the maths, Nina will think, later, clarity gifted by distance. There is no way she cannot have known, cannot have aligned the handing of two tablets of paracetamol to her student over breakfast on the trip to Cork to the facts of six months later. Nina had not even looked for help that morning. She was clearly in need. Miss Lambert had seen this. Miss Lambert was kind. Not at all teacher-like. Miss Lambert had jollied her along, and this had made Nina feel even worse.

'We've all been there, Nina,' she'd smiled. 'Don't feel bad, you're only human.'

Up at the breakfast bar, spooning scrambled eggs and picking sausage and rashers onto his plate with a tongs, was the man Nina had seen Miss Lambert with the night before.

Nina is used to boy energy, but her brothers are a different breed of human to this Mark. She watches as he paints below the newly installed dado rail, the rough handling of his roller, the rough cut of his head. A double crown, from which hair whorls randomly, as if he has cut it himself. And probably he has. His motion is constant, Nina can't imagine him sitting still long enough for a barber to do a decent job.

As she watches, the baby kicks into her ribs. Hard. And she thinks, with curiosity more than panic: What if my baby is a boy like this boy? How would I cope? To be mother to such a child when I am barely past childhood myself? Who would be there to help?

'He's a good lad really,' Father Tarran says, filling up the paint tray next to her. 'No harm in him.'

They look at the boy who is applying paint to the wall with effort, the energy required for concentration on the task breaking from him in waves, filling the room with an edge of unease. Filling Nina with unease, thoughts she needs distracting from.

'Miss Lambert says you're from around here?'

'I used to live in this house,' Father Tarran says, pouring more paint into his own tray. 'For a time. We rented it. My father was director of St. Columba's Hospital, they were renovating the house there and we needed somewhere to stay. We were here for a little over a year, when I was twelve.'

Nina tries to picture what the man might have looked like as a child, a boy in shorts and tee shirt, runners. Struggles. He seems so set in himself. Like he has always been an adult.

'Do you have brothers and sisters?'

'No, just me. Only child.'

'You must have been lonely, in such a huge house.'

Nina is often lonely at home, in a house not quite the size of this one, even with all the attendant comings and goings and noise of three siblings.

'I suppose I was,' he says. 'There was a gang of local lads I hung out with. Mark reminds me of one of them. Larry was his name.'

'What happened to him?'

She knows as she says it the question could be considered pointed, looks at Mark, avoids Father Tarran's eye.

'I don't know,' he says. In a way that makes her think he does.

Nina thinks about boys. Her mother used to say she would raise ten girls rather than another one. Wonders about the boy who is about to become the father of her baby. He doesn't know this. Will likely never know this. Even if she wanted to tell him, she can't. Would find it hard to pick him out in a line-up. Oh, she could, if she wanted, try to narrow it down. She knows he was from one of the midland schools. There weren't many of them, but her head was so obscured with drink and hurt and confusion she barely registered his name. Can't pinpoint if it was John or Paul, one or the other. Maybe he even gave her a false name, passed it to her with a swig of Southern Comfort from his hip flask, a puff of his rollie, which may, or may not, have been tobacco. He is nameless. He is almost faceless. And it blows Nina's mind to think his DNA, co-mingled with hers, might wander the earth and him unaware. The act itself seemed inconsequential.

Mrs Kelly calls them for a lunch of Oxtail soup and day old bread rolls, laid out on the kitchen counter.

'That's me done,' the woman says, removing her apron. 'Fr Tarran says you're getting fish and chips for dinner.'

An almost-look on Fr Tarran's face tells Nina this was meant as a surprise.

'I have to go out now too,' he says. 'You're free for the

afternoon, but don't wander too far if you go out. Stick together. I'll be back by about six. Siobhán, you're in charge.'

Nina watches the priest as he eyes Mark, his face unreadable, ruffles the boy's hair, readies himself to leave.

It's icy in the kitchen, the heating, it turns out, is only on for short spurts of time to save money, or to impress visitors like Miss Lambert, Siobhán tells Nina.

'She's very pretty, your teacher.'

Nina nods, the crust of the should-be-soft breadroll cracking and flaking at the corners of her mouth.

'I think Father Tarran likes her.'

'He's a priest.'

'He's a man.'

Nina feels protective towards her teacher, as if she should warn her, which is ridiculous. Warn her of what? It is she who is in an altered reality. Miss Lambert is safe back within the walls of St Eithne's.

Nina feels a sharp longing for the curve of the hall into the convent building, terrazzo tiling and high windows. The music room, with its random lecterns, the piano, strewn and stacked with sheets of music. First year, when she harboured ambitions of playing the cello. Her mother had discouraged it.

'A cello would be too big for you Nina. A woodwind would be more appropriate. Have you considered the Oboe? Even the piano. At least they're in situ, you wouldn't have to cart it about on a bus.'

Miss Lambert plays the cello. And the piano, and the oboe, and most woodwind instruments. She sings too, a beautiful sweet soprano, but not as beautiful as Nina's voice. Even in all her modesty, Nina knows she is gifted. Can call to mind in a moment the thrill she felt the day Miss Lambert stopped the choir, asked them to sing individually so that she could pick out who she was hearing. Nina had feared her range was too limited, her projection was off, but the look on her teacher's face told her this was far from the case. As she climbed the register of Ave Maria towards the highest notes, Nina felt like a witch casting a spell. A power deep and resident within her she did not know she possessed.

'Did I hear you say you sing?' Siobhán says.
'A bit.'
'I'd love to be able to sing.'
'Everybody can sing.'
As she says it she can hear Miss Lambert say to her, in the confines of the music room:
'I really do believe everybody can sing with training, Nina, but your voice is exceptional. Any effort we put in here will pay huge dividends. I think we can already start you working towards trials for the Royal Irish Academy or the Cork School of Music.'

Fridays became her favourite day, not for the reason they were for others, the end of the week, but because she had double music in the morning, followed by one-on-one voice coaching with Miss Lambert after school. Sunlight refracting through the wibbly panes of the music room window, rainbow hues, streaking her teacher's face, her long ringless fingers, the piano keys dancing as they hit notes perfectly upon repeat. Cocooned in a world of two, floating high towards the ceiling, the cracked plasterwork. Alchemy in the room, her tiny body a tornado of emotion.

'I play the piano, a little,' Siobhán says, shyly.

There's something starved about the girl's face. Not a lack of weight. A lack of other nourishment. Something else. A glimmer of joy and pride Nina recognises. A shadow belief in her ability to do something well.

'There's one here. In the front room. I could play and you could sing a little if you like?'

'Sure why not?' Nina says.

'Mark, you come with us,' Siobhán says, smiling back. Her energy changed. All of their energy changed as they tidy away the lunch things, head to the living room, still fusty and scattered with cardboard boxes from elsewhere.

'Donations,' Siobhán says, noticing Nina's gaze. 'We're the local charity shop.'

'Can I open one?' Mark says. 'Please, Siobhán, please, please?'

'It's like Christmas every day for Mark in here,' Siobhán says. 'Just one, Mark. And mind you put whatever you take out of it away on the shelves, don't make a mess.'

Mark grins. Sticks out his tongue. Siobhán swats him.

'You're a Holy Terror,' she says.

He takes a box from behind a sofa and starts pulling duct tape from it. Noisily. Removes a soft toy, a tired looking Tigger, a game of Connect 4, some books. He opens the Connect 4, puts it on the coffee table, starts to construct it.

'That'll keep him happy for hours,' Siobhán says to Nina.

The piano is old, a Steinway, similar to the one in school, but worn with woodworm, ringed from abandoned mugs and plates. The stool looks like it has come from a bar.

'Is it tuned?' Nina says.

'It is. Father Tarran plays a little too. He had it done a few weeks ago. Maybe, when we have more people here, we can have our own little band.'

Nina smiles at the thought. The image. A new tribe. A gang of raggle-taggle trouble-making troubadours, making music on the edge of Ireland.

'We could call ourselves The Castouts,' she says.

Siobhán looks at her.

'You won't be cast out,' she says, softly. Kindly. 'You'll have your baby and go back and nobody will know a thing.'

A wave of sadness off the girl, which Nina would like to explore, ask about, but she senses she won't get a straightforward answer.

'Would you like to sing 'Imagine?' Siobhán says.

'Sure.'

Siobhán sits on the wobbly stool, places her feet on the pedals, opens the lid and readies her fingers. As she strokes the keys with practiced competence, Nina's voice rises and the room is transformed. Mark, breaks from his solitaire game of Connect 4 to clap the final notes.

'Bravo! Bravo!' he says.

Nina smiles at Siobhán.

'You're good,' she says.

And the girl's face lights.

'Another?'

The baby in Nina's tummy kicks so hard its movement is visible through her tee shirt.

'I think he's demanding it.'

They find their groove in a medley of Elton John and Billy Joel and dwindling December afternoon light and by the time they've gotten to Journey and Don't Stop Believin', it is nearly dark.

'You sing so beautifully,' Siobhán says. And Nina feels

something akin to happiness for the first time she can remember in a long time.

'Where's Mark?' she says.

They look to the sofa, but the boy is not there.

'Oh shit,' Siobhán says.

They make their way to the kitchen, Siobhán turning on lights as they go.

'Mark?' she calls. 'Mark?'

Nina spots him through the half glass kitchen door, sat on a bench in the garden. He's wearing only the tee shirt from earlier, and it is freezing. He's playing a game with the Tigger and a Pooh which might have come from the same box or a previous one. The toys are fighting with each other.

'Come in from there, Mark,' Siobhán says. 'You'll catch your death, love.'

Mark obeys. Slopes back in through the door with a grin. He clearly likes Siobhán. Trusts her.

'Go upstairs and get yourself a jumper,' she says. 'I'm going to put the kettle on. See if that auld bitch Kelly left us any biscuits.'

She busies herself at the sink. Nina fetches plates and cups and milk and sugar. They sit in the harsh electric light at the oilcloth covered table, its chips and exposed seams grubby from wear.

'He's a good lad,' Siobhán says. 'His father drinks. Hits him. That's why he won't go home. Can't go home.'

Nina thinks of her own brothers, her mother, her father, shouting at them, discharging threats and justice for mild misdoings. They would never strike them. The thought of it would be alien to them. Nina feels sad for Mark. For all sweet Marks, for all their sadnesses.

'You're very kind to him. You and Father Tarran.'

'Well, Father Tarran says kindness will always get you where you want to go quicker.'

There is warmth in Siobhán's voice. For the first time, Nina feels like she might be okay here. She might be safe here.

'What about you?' she says. 'Why are you living here now?'

Hesitation on the young woman's face. A long pause.

'I was teaching,' she says. 'Small primary school. In Caherciveen. They fired me. I didn't take it well, I guess. Ended up a bit of a mess with drink. With drugs.'

She stops, as if lost in a memory.

'I'm sorry,' Nina says. And she is. Sorry she has asked. Afraid she has destroyed the happy moment. The pain etched on the woman's face is deep, unknowable to her, and she can think of no other words to express solidarity, to salve it.

'It's okay. The local priest knew Father Tarran, knew about this place. I came here. I was lucky.' Siobhán says.

'Why did they fire you?'

Siobhán stills, as if she is thinking how to answer. Whether to answer. Again, Nina is sorry to have asked the question. Would give anything to hear, beyond the crescendo tick of the kitchen clock, Father Tarran's key in the front door.

'They said I was a pervert. Not to be trusted with children.'

Nina tries to control her features, arrange them in sympathy. Feels surprise, disbelief, confusion.

'A pervert?'

'I fell in love with a woman,' Siobhán says.

Nina has no reference for lesbianism past bathroom scrawls 'Antoinette McCormack is a lezzer', 'Mary and Claire, in a tree, K-I-S-S-I-N-G'. *The Hunger*, with Catherine Deneuve and Susan Sarandon, which her mother wouldn't let her go see, which the girls who had seen talked about in hushed tones, as if they were privy to a dangerous secret. Looking at Siobhán, she feels she should say something, wants to say something, but no words seem appropriate and the ones that come to mind are stupid: 'Do you like being a lesbian?', 'Do people know?', 'Do you hate boys?'.

Mark comes back into the kitchen and Siobhán pours tea, gives him a couple of Fig Rolls. Pats him on the shoulder, compliments his jumper.

'Can I open another box?' he says.

'Go on then,' she says. 'Just the one, mind.'

The boy departs. Siobhán doesn't hate boys. Her eyes are kind. She would make a good mother, Nina thinks. And the sad, never far away, reaches for her again.

'You won't have children, then?' she says.

Siobhán shrugs.

'Who knows, Nina. The woman I loved had children, was married, was older. But no, I don't think I will.'

'She was married?'

Siobhán shrugs.

'It wasn't a choice, Nina. I felt what I felt. She felt it too. When I was with her, it was like I was … maybe for the first time, properly alive? Myself? I can't explain it.'

Siobhán looks flustered, sad. As if she is seeking kindness, understanding and is not confident she deserves it.

Nina puts her hands out, lays them on the table, as if to steady herself. As if to steady the world. As if the illusion of safety she felt only moments ago is disintegrating into fine particles of dust. Reforming into a tornado.

'What happened to her?' Nina says.

'She's living her life.'

'You're not together?'

'No. It got complicated. She didn't want to be associated with me, after all the fuss. Didn't want her children to know.'

'But do you still love her?'

'I do.'

Nina watches the scene as if from above. The two of them sitting there, two ordinary young women, strong tea and custard creams, bathed in harsh yellow light, heartbeats, thoughts, maybe, pulsing to the ticking of the clock.

Nina thinks about love. About the baby within her, strong with new life. She knows she already loves him. She supposes, despite everything, she must love her parents, her siblings. But she knows too that the kind of love Siobhán is talking about is different. Wild. Uncontrollable. Painful. A love without choice. Love which rises like music on a Friday afternoon, pitch perfect notes crashing on raddled window panes, rattling them, shattering them in sweet explosion. Love so passionate that seeing the object of your longing in the arms of another human could be your undoing. And she thinks this: she has never looked at a boy and wanted desperately to hold him, to kiss him, to press herself into the folds of him. To lose herself in his self, in his smell. No, this love Siobhán is referring to. Nina has never felt this. Not for a boy.

4: 1999

ELIZABETH

In the room of swirling carpets and after his offer of tea and Kimberley Mikados, Father Hyland introduces the priest sitting in the armchair next to the bay window.

'Elizabeth, this is Fr Pearce. He's stationed out in San Francisco, and home for a visit like yourself.'

Father Hyland had mentioned him when I first went to study at Stanford. He works with the community in the Mission District but spends most of his time pursuing interests outside the Church, offering outstanding odds, sure bets and three-way specials on racetracks around the State of California.

'Father Pearce, this is Elizabeth, Mrs Kelly's daughter. She received a scholarship a couple of years ago for Stanford. We're very proud of her,' he says, raising his blue willow teacup towards me in a toast.

I owe the scholarship opportunity to Father Hyland, who had encouraged my academic endeavours and arranged private tutoring. He believes in what I'm doing, unlike my own father who thinks it's a waste of time.

Father Pearce smiles and shakes my hand enthusiastically. His fingers are pale and plump, and carefully manicured. His eyes zone in on me, taking in my plaid flannel shirt over a Nirvana tee shirt and baggy jeans.

'That's fantastic, young lady. Well done. And what are you studying?'

'Computer engineering – programming, algorithms, software technologies – that kind of thing.'

'Well, speaking of technology,' Father Hyland says, 'Father Pearce was telling me that he's moved on from the action at Golden Gate Fields to shares in Silicon Valley.' He laughs softly and nudges Father Pearce, 'Go on then, give her the spiel on your big idea.'

Like the sharing of sacred bread, Father Pearce quietly passes me a piece of cardboard. I, in turn, refrain from the impulse to bless myself and examine what appears to be the back of a Cornflakes box, taking in the words Pets.com. The .com part underlined several times.

As a form of explanation, he strides up to the top of the room and launches into a short sermon which takes inspiration from the miracle of five loaves and two fishes.

'For a modest investment, the likely returns would grow and feed the multitudes, so to speak,' he says, nostrils flaring, his fervour tempered by Father Hyland's head shaking and sporadic tutting. Father Pearce wraps up his sermon and it feels like the closing stages of Mass when the air is lighter and there is a sense of relief that it's almost over.

'What do you think?' Father Pearce asks me.

'I hear about technology companies all the time around campus. Rumours about the next company about to skyrocket, but it's all a bit of a gamble.'

'Exactly what I've been telling him,' Father Hyland says. 'This particular one is a dead cert,' he tells us. 'The form is unbelievable.'

Once back in the States, I input the data from the Financial Times and The Wall Street Journal, and I'm quite pleased with myself when the computer screen shows a simple table with the staggering trajectory of the Pets.com shares. Wow. I triple-check the financial figures. The shares had quintupled in value over the past twelve months. It isn't guess-work or assumptions on my part, it's factual data from reliable sources.

In an email to Father Hyland, I relay my findings. The results are met with a slice of his usual scepticism. He informs me that Father Pearce has lost the run of himself while attending the Bishops' Conference in Maynooth. Under the shade of the Silken Thomas Yew, secrets from Silicon Valley were revealed to pot-bellied bishops, with Father Pearce counting and recounting the unstoppable gallop of dot-com stock.

Along with ecumenical matters, an idea forms under the collective mitres of the bishops' central command, and it receives an unofficial blessing from the archbishop. Father Pearce becomes the middleman for a diocese-level investment scheme. Each diocese has discretion to choose its own stock and each reports separately on incomings and outgoings. I imagine there was much swilling of sacramental wine as the investment value ballooned.

I return to my studies and work hard, but the pressure here is intense. Everyone is an A student; everything is a competition. I worry it might not be for me. In the haze of dorm parties and assignments and assessments, I forget about the investment scheme until I receive some unexpected news in an email from my mother.

Dear Elizabeth,

I hope you are doing well and keeping your head down now that the exams are coming up.

A bit of news from my side, our lovely Father Hyland is heading over to San Francisco on the 14th. He decided to go all of a sudden. Maybe you could arrange to meet him?

It's been hectic here making plans for Monksfield House after refurbishment plans were announced. The diocese must have come into a nice bit of money as the bishop instructed Father Hyland to order a Carrara marble altar for the church. It weighs over seven tonnes, bless us and save us. It's due to arrive in time for the new millennium and will be unveiled by the bishop himself.

I'll send over a little package for you with Father Hyland. Your usual favourites.

Love, Mam

I meet Father Hyland at the airport, his tall frame and fair hair marking him out from the other passengers as he walks through Arrivals. However, there's something different about him. A weariness has settled upon him, like a water-weary fisherman off the boat at Killybegs. Not at all the man I know. On the cab ride from the airport, he fills me in on the latest developments.

'Father Pearce contacted me, lamenting the downturn in the stock and babbling on and on about a black swan . I've known him a long time, going back twenty years when we entered the Sem together, and I've never heard him so hysterical.'

I wonder how these two have remained friends over the years, their personalities inversely correlated, their energies travelling different circuits but overlapping from time to time.

Father Hyland is quiet and slumps against the side of the cab, staring out as we travel along Route 101. I offer to accompany him to his meeting with Father Pearce. He agrees, reluctantly, saying that I have a better head for figures than he has, and that a second opinion might be prudent.

After he settles into his accommodation, he receives a call from Father Pearce's housekeeper who arranges for us to be collected and brought to the rectory. She serves us tea and key lime pie on arrival. The men speak quietly while I sit on the leather couch and gaze at the paintings on the wall which look like Caravaggio masterpieces. There are no masterpieces hanging on the damp walls of Monksfield House. I wonder about the fate of priests and their assigned parishes. How one ends up in an ageing mansion in a soggy field off the west coast of Ireland and another ends up in the beating centre of the Golden State.

Father Hyland's voice rises, and his face is now a flustered pink, 'I have people already hired to work on the house. Pat Sheahan's crew are doing the roofing and Jim Canty is doing the electrics. These people need to be paid. Martin, these people must be paid.'

Father Hyland walks across the room and hands me the printouts Father Pearce had given him.

'Look at that. Those figures. It's an absolute mess,' he says.

I flick through the pages. There are figures for investments in different companies. I scan the pages again, adding in my head as I go, my heart rate rises. It looks like… yes it appears to run into the millions of dollars by May, and by October the value of the stock had plummeted... seven, then ten times less than the peak. How could that happen in a matter of months?

I look at the backs of the priests who are now huddled over a notepad which Father Pearce is aggressively attacking with a pen.

'So where did all the money come from?' I ask.

Father Pearce stops, sighs, and then says quietly, 'The Bishop's Council gave the go-ahead to combine the funds from various dioceses.'

'So, you're saying the original investment put in by the bishops, noted here at ten million dollars, was taken from parish funds? This money was donated to the Church by parishioners?'

As my brain computes the average bounty collected in round reed baskets across the parishes of Ireland, Father Hyland looks away and puts his head in his hands. Father Pearce takes out the Waterford Crystal decanter and pours a whiskey for himself and Father Hyland and offers me more tea. He raises his glass tumbler to the crucifix on the wall.

'Well, it's Church money as such, and the bishops are entitled to do with it as they see fit,' he says.

I top up my tea with the whiskey from the decanter and raise my cup to the crucifix. Father Hyland looks my way but refrains from commenting.

Mrs O'Neill, the housekeeper, knocks and enters the room again and speaks to Father Pearce quietly. His face darkens as if something hellish has entered the room alongside her.

'Well,' he says, after she leaves, 'the Bull, remember him, that eejit from Sligo who was made bishop after his brief stint in the Congo? He has made plans to visit and will be here tomorrow.'

Father Hyland, obviously aware of said Bull, downs his whiskey. I feel like I'm caught in the middle of a movie mishmash where Father Ted stars in The Field.

'We cannot be held responsible for the vagaries of the stock market. It was the Bishops' Council directing the investments. I advised them to spread the risk,' Father Pearce says, and stands then as if suddenly inspired. 'I will not be held accountable for their mismanagement,' and striding towards the door, he says, 'Terry, I have some matters to attend to.'

Before Father Hyland has time to comment, Father Pearce is out the gap. We both sit for a few moments in unsettled silence before ordering a cab.

> Dear Elizabeth,
>
> I'm not sure what's going on but a few days after Father Hyland left for the States, two men arrived from the seminary in Maynooth and went about questioning the staff.
>
> They didn't devote much time to me. They don't realise the information I glean about people while I clean. You know well the types of incidents I've had to deal with in Monksfield, and some were shocking to me, never mind soft-handed men who have spent years hidden away in the sanctuary of St. Patrick's in Maynooth. Not that I would ever tell a soul about the guests here.
>
> The men spent a lot of time with Maggie, looking through the files in the office. She told them that she didn't have any dealings with parish funds, only general house supplies and petty cash. She was rightly cheesed off and packed them off to Casey, the bookkeeper

in town, and by all accounts, they were given the road by him, too.

The rumour mills have started to turn and let's just say certain accusations are being made against Father Hyland. A delivery of paint and timber was on the way up to the house when we were told not to accept it as the bill would not be paid, and I had to deal with a very irate Galway man when I asked him to cancel the order for new pews.

Do you know what's going on? Please ask Father Hyland to phone and let us know.

Love, Mam

I meet Father Hyland the next day at his accommodation and tell him about Mam's email.

'Isn't she a great woman using the modern technology,' he says, staring impassively out the window at the cable cars cruising along Lombard Street, 'I'll phone her after I deal with the Bull.'

I point to various articles in the newspapers I've brought from Stanford library. The first inkling that market conditions were changing was hidden in the small print of The Wall Street Journal. A number of small technology companies had gone bankrupt after they ran out of cash. These were dismissed as anomalies with mentions of misguided business plans. Others followed. The news had been lost in the maelstrom of the millennium bug.

'Any sign of Father Pearce? ' I ask.

'No, he hasn't returned to the rectory. I've contacted several known associates, but the only lead as to his whereabouts is from a volunteer down at a shelter in the Mission District.

She says he's gone to Baker's Beach. Some of his advisors are based down there.'

I wait a moment to see if further information is forthcoming but there is none.

'Advisors?'

'He knows people.'

Father Hyland shrugs and I fail to read whether there is more to understand from his comment. For some reason I think of the Godfather but dismiss the idea. He looks at his watch. I recall my mother saying that Father Hyland knows many things about many people, things they wish to keep hidden. I wonder about the confessional of swallowed secrets and how he manages to contain it.

'I don't have time to go to the beach before the Bull arrives so I'm just going to have to make my way over to the rectory and go there afterwards.'

'I'll go with you. I've a brown belt in karate. You know… if the Bull tries anything funny.'

I launch into a twist kick, followed by an imaginary swish of a bullfighter's muleta, and detect a tiny smile.

'Ok, ok. I know you're going to plague me until I agree. You can come and chat to Mrs O'Neill and see if she knows who Father Pearce might be meeting at Baker's Beach.'

A booming deep voice signals the arrival of the Bull, and it isn't long before cross words rise from the sitting room. The sound of a fist on a table and something falling to the ground. I consider going in but then I hear the door open and the Bull storms out.

'Two days to sort this fiasco out, and God help you after that.'

Father Hyland comes into the kitchen after the Bull's onslaught. He moves his shoulders in circles and then his head from side-to-side, stretching his neck muscles like a rugby player after a rough tackle.

'Members from the Bishops' Council will arrive in three days. They appear to be aware of the decline in the stock but not quite the scale of the disaster.'

'What are you going to do?' I ask.

'Pray. And find Pearce.'

As we approach the beach, I notice a large number of people milling around just beyond the boardwalk entrance. The sun is setting over the Bay Area and the fluorescent patterns on the beachgoers clothing is beginning to show. A small woman in dungarees is passing out glow sticks and neon sunglasses.

'I've heard about these,' I say, 'It looks like they're setting up for a rave.'

Father Hyland repeats the word rave and mutters something about having met a few stragglers coming from a rave on the back beach at home. I scan the crowd but it's difficult to identify individuals amongst the swarm.

'How will we find Father Pearce in a place like this?'

'Someone will know who he's with. It's hard to hide a priest,' he says.

He touches his clerical collar, running his finger across the white insert that glows in the disco lights. We decide to split up and I wade through the crowd, stopping now and then to ask after Father Pearce. A teenager wearing a multi-coloured basketball hat and matching fanny pack offers me a small tub of jellybeans and a bottle of water. I hand him $20 and wait for change but he moves off into the crowd.

The DJ turns up the beat as the sun slips below the horizon. I feel each thump of bass in my chest. The rhythm crawls along my rib cage. The crowd are waving glow sticks in the air; someone passes one to me, and I raise it above my head to meet the others. The greens and pinks appear in waves as the music rises and falls. I look at the sky and see that the stars are now visible. How can we trust the stars? Those stars could be dead now, but we see them twinkling above us. I hear the nursery rhyme and sing along… twinkle, twinkle, little nothing. Can we trust anyone… not Father Pearce, definitely not him…or the big bad bishop bullman, not him… anyone? Jesus…are you up there…hello…earth calling Jesus…come in Jesus…

I start to laugh and a guy next to me kisses me. It feels so good. 'Rhythm Is a Dancer' comes on and I see Father Hyland up on a stand near the DJ, wearing a neon band on his head and his collar flashes green and red in time to the beat. Muzzing around he waves his hands in the air. Another dancer joins him, but I can't see him clearly. I wonder if it's Father Pearce.

I feel a hand on my shoulder and turn. It's Father Hyland. He speaks but I can't make out what he is saying over the music, so we move off beyond the crowd towards the boardwalk.

'Are you ok?' he asks.

'Why?'

'You're soaked.'

I feel my clothes. They are indeed wet. I look at him. No halo. No flashing collar.

'Some guy threw his water bottle over me.'

I laugh, rub my arms, sprinkling sand on our shoes.

'I thought you said you wouldn't take those anymore.'

'What? Jellybeans?'

Father Hyland sighs. I feel like hugging him, but memory intercepts and serves me up an embossed image of my ecstasy vomit on the grey slate tiles of his kitchen floor. My mother's eternal embarrassment presses upon me, compressing me. They would never understand how I need to take my mind away from itself every now and then.

'Let's go. I have what I need,' he says.

'So, you found Father Pearce?' I ask.

'No, but I know he's not here.'

```
Dear Elizabeth,

I haven't heard anything from yourself or
Father Hyland and I'm beginning to worry.
Please let me know that you are ok, pet. My
mind is running wild imagining what's going on
over there.

Things are getting worse at home. The clerics
from Maynooth were on to their superiors,
after which they told us not to answer the
phone or open any post. Then off they flew
like bats on a night hunt and were later seen
entering the solicitor's house.

By morning, the town had it that there was a
large hole in the parish finances and fingers
were pointing to Father Hyland. His unexplained
absence doesn't help matters. Maggie heard
that he was sunning himself on the deck of
a Mediterranean cruise ship on foot of their
weekly offerings. The rubbish some people will
believe, not to mention they are raking up
the past. The rumours about his love affair
with that married woman in Zambia, and his
disgraced return, are doing the rounds again.
```

```
I also heard that concerns have been raised
about Monksfield House and the type of guests
who stay with us. People are saying they'll be
transferred to the Mental. I don't know what
to do. Sure, they wouldn't last a week there.

Please phone me if you can. I'm home every
evening now.

Love, Mam
```

Father Hyland ignores me on the cab ride home from the beach, except to mention that it might be best if I extricate myself from the situation. I briefly consider this option and think of my small room at Aspen dorms. The computer takes up half the room, my books another quarter and I squeeze into the remaining quarter. I soak up everything the university has to offer; the lectures, the study, assignments, optional credits – it allows me to stretch and flex my mind. I look at Father Hyland again and feel that I should, at least, try to help.

The next day, I meet him in the breakfast room of his accommodation and ask about Father Pearce.

'He's flown the nest,' he says, his voice just above a whisper.

'What do you mean?'

'He booked three one-way tickets to different destinations.'

I watch him pour maple syrup onto his pancakes and add sugar to his coffee. He stirs it repeatedly with a small spoon.

'Spreading his risk,' I say, after I figure out the reason for multiple flights.

'I'm sure he'll come forward when he has time to reflect,' Father Hyland adds, even though I can tell he doesn't believe the words himself. He looks desolate then, like a man banished to the desert to seek meaning, knowing he will never find it.

'So, you're going to take the rap and face the Council on your own?'

'That appears to be the current state of play,' he says.

He places a large forkful of pancake in his mouth signalling that this is the end of the discussion on the matter. I ignore the signal and suggest that we should gather any letters and documents related to the investments and ensure that we have evidence of Father Pearce's involvement and the instructions from the bishops.

'There's no need for that. Everything is above board, and the truth will out in the end,' he says.

Still, after everything he has seen, he retains his faith in the ecclesiastical pyramid of priests propping up the bishops, and the Church, all the way up to a perfect point in the sky. I decide to take it upon myself to search Father Pearce's residence for evidence and send word to my mother to do the same at Monksfield House.

```
Dear Elizabeth,

I felt a sudden weakness after our phone call
yesterday. I just can't believe they took money
from the people of this parish and squandered
it.

Many families here have been reeling since the
summer when they invested the bit of money they
had in Eircom and that was a major flop. And
now this.
```

> The clerics have already searched Father
> Hyland's room, but I suspect they didn't know
> about the files he kept in the garden shed.
> Since Easter he has taken to birdwatching, and
> from the window there he can see the gulls and
> kittiwakes hover and plunge into the waves. I
> came across him only a few weeks ago and we
> talked for a while looking out at the wild
> Atlantic. He told me the sea draws pain from
> us and somehow flattens it out, and that's
> why Monksfield House was such a good place
> for the young and needy, it offered a kind of
> a comfort just by being next to it. There is
> certainly some truth in what he said.
>
> I've gathered whatever correspondence I can,
> and I have it stored safely here in case you
> need it. I hope it will be of help.
>
> I have been thinking that maybe it would be
> best for you to return to college and get your
> head back into the books. Father Hyland will
> have to manage this mess on his own. We can
> only do so much.
>
> Love, Mam

Father Hyland allows me to accompany him to the meeting with the Bull and bishops.

'Your presence may dull the knives they wield, I suppose,' Father Hyland says, blessing himself.

I had only ever met a bishop once at my Confirmation, and he was a gentle man with a crosier curved spine. Father Hyland's demeanour signals that these men are of a different breed.

'I am also a witness should things turn... you know...' I tell him.

I didn't really know how it could turn. These bishops are not serious criminals who would bundle Father Hyland into a car and throw him over the Golden Gate Bridge, at least I didn't think so. I take it upon myself to arrange for one of the PhD students in college, Conor Aiken, to attend the meeting also. I had to disclose more than I wanted to about the pickle we were in, but to a guy like him it's market regulation and behaviour he's interested in rather than the religious leanings of the investors.

At the appointed time on the third day, four thin bishops wearing long black coats file into the rectory dining room, more Matrix than Maynooth. They sit at one side of the table, and open identical leather briefcases. Folders are extracted and files open. No handshakes are offered in salutation only curt commands from the Bull.

Aiken stands and opens proceedings by explaining why a series of rare and unpredictable events resulted in major losses in the market, how the stocks were overheated and had they taken a more prudent approach their losses could have been reduced, although they still would have taken a significant hit. I watch his hands as he gesticulates and recall the feel of those hands on the flat of my tummy, along my back, opening my bra, feeling my breast. His theories are dismissed by the wave of an episcopal-ringed pinkie.

The roaring Bull attacks us with full force, but this time Father Hyland moves gracefully to one side and avoids the rush of his rage. Something in him seems to have altered. He answers their questions in a quiet monotone, almost impatient to get to the end of it. In a matter-of-fact way he mentions the correspondence that evidences their instructions.

The bishops respond with threats of excommunication and exile, confinement, and curtailment of duties, as if somehow these things would reverse their financial damnation.

In the end Father Hyland stands, 'Do what you will. I have acted with integrity and for the good of the congregation. The decisions on the investments came from you. I was merely following orders passing the offerings along. My actions will be judged by the Lord, and ultimately yours will too. There has been no impropriety on my part.'

The Bull blocks the door. Aiken and I pick up the cue from Father Hyland to make an attempt to leave.

'Step aside, Sir,' Aiken says, staring down the Bull.

The Bull pauses momentarily, possibly calculating the societal capital afforded to a Stanfordite, and then moves aside allowing us to leave.

Father Hyland says nothing, absolutely nothing, on the cab ride back to his lodgings. Their attack has silenced him. Abandoned by Father Pearce and blamed by the bishops, it must be hard for him.

I quiz Aiken on options to address their fiscal mismanagement of parish funds.

'Once the money has moved from parishioner to priest – it becomes theirs. And so technically it was theirs to do with as they please. There is no case to answer,' he says.

'Except the moral one,' I say, looking over at Father Hyland and noting the sorrow in his silence. I have failed to help the man who has done so much for me.

'Morals don't come into it,' Aiken says. He shrugs. A closed case, as far as he is concerned.

He's right. The scale of this financial disaster will be concealed. There will be no Garda investigation, no atonement, no penance. There would be consequences for Father Hyland of course. The injustice of it sits in my stomach and sours.

Dear Elizabeth,

I was glad to hear that you are back at your lectures at the university. I haven't seen Father Hyland since he returned from the States. Word has it that he took a turn when he learned that the guests had been moved to other accommodation. I had been up at the house myself helping them to pack. It was an awful sight. One poor lad, John, in tears, having come here after three foster homes, told to move again. The clerics rushing to-and-fro, boxing items. There was no compassion, Elizabeth, there really wasn't. I wouldn't be surprised if Father Hyland gave up on the Church altogether after this. He spent a lot of time questioning the actions of the Church after that television documentary States of Fear, not to mention the Father Brendan Smyth case a few years ago.

We were told that Monksfield house was unsafe, and it would close until further notice. It's no more unsafe than it was for the last few years. There's a rumour going around that it will be used as a home for retired priests, but who knows whether there's any truth in that.

There will be work cleaning the holiday homes next summer, and I might pick up something in the new estate up at Uaimh Farraige. Apparently, most of the houses have been bought by blow-ins and they hire (and fire) on a regular basis. I'm not sure what I'll do really, something about the whole saga has left me out of sorts. I suppose I feel let down by those I trusted.

Around town, people are bad-mouthing Father Hyland, as if they don't remember all the good he has done for others. I try to stick up for him and tell them the problem with the funds wasn't his doing, but sometimes people don't want to listen. They want someone to blame.

There's talk that he'll be sent overseas. It would be an awful loss to the community if you ask me, but others disagree. Eaten bread is soon forgotten! God knows he'll have an awful time of it if he stays here and he's hung out to dry for missing parish funds. We know that he doesn't always toe the party line but that's his nature, he can't help it. It's like the sea, it ebbs and flows no matter the obstacle. That's its nature. His nature is to do what he thinks is right – no matter the consequences.

I worry about you so far away. Do your best with your studies.

Love, Mam x

5: 2007

THE CASEYS

Two girls came bounding down the stairs in a fit of exasperated laughter.

'Bye, Ma! Bye, Da!' called out one, plaited hair swinging behind her. She let out a string of words lost in the shrieking 'I'm telling you' of her friend, closed the back door with a little too much force, causing the cutlery to rattle on the draining board.

'Who was that, Car?' Mark Casey asked his wife, who was rising from his lap.

'Becca,' said Carmel, giving her husband a swipe of a tea towel. 'How do you not know her name by now, you eejit.'

'What?'

'She's always here. Sure, she was here only last week.'

'She was?'

'For Em's birthday?'

'Oh yeah.'

'Poor thing. I don't think she gets on very well with her father, you know.'

Mark picked up a toothpick from the white porcelain cube on the table, jemmied it around his mouth. He had just polished off a plate of scrambled eggs, black and white pudding, three slices of toast smothered in butter. A few rashers wouldn't have gone amiss, but he wasn't going to mention it.

'Why, who's her father?'

'Mick McGrath.'

'From up there beside Grange?'

'Yeah, that's him.'

'Bit of a cunt alright.'

'Mark!'

'Sorry. Bit of an old so-and-so alright. You know yours is the only cu—'

'Mark!'

'C'mere to me.' Mark reached out to grab his wife's waist. Carmel laughed.

'You'll be late,' she said and, as if on cue, Mark's phone rang, making Carmel jump. 'That bloody thing.'

Mark rose, saying, 'yeah, yeah, yeah,' down the phone while manoeuvring his foot into one shoe, then the other.

'Don't forget,' Carmel called after him as he put an arm through his jacket by the back door. He moved his head away from the phone, covered the top of it with his palm.

'What, Car,' said Mark, a twinge of irritation in his voice.

'I'm away to Siobhan's later, won't be home tonight.'

Mark set his jaw and furrowed his brow as he took this information in. 'Toby?'

'Coming with me,' Carmel said and Mark smiled with a nod, gave his wife a two-finger salute as he turned on his heel and headed out the door.

The daylight hit Mark like a slap in the face as soon as his feet met the herringbone laneway. He got off the phone with a gravelly, 'On my way,' grateful for Clarky calling when he did. He was battling the effects of the night before and had immediately regretted initiating anything with Carmel. She'd have been up for it and all, that wild thing.

It was just, at that particular moment, as his wife caressed his face at the kitchen table, the stark memory of that Polish midget belly dancing on the table of Spark's nightclub came muscling its way into his mind. Carmel having, he noticed, the exact same blondie hair as that midget. With the roots. Carmel never usually let her roots grow out like that.

The drive to work was pierced with memories of the night before. The midget, what was her name again? Laura? No, Lara. With the little pot belly on her, shaking those hips with the red bra, thrown in Mark's general direction, the golden coin belt going jingle jangle. She'd brought out a bright yellow boa constrictor at one point. How she had the strength to hold the thing around her neck, or how she didn't trip up over it. The thing must have been six foot long at least. How did they even get a snake into the club?

A car horn blasted and Mark jumped. Shit, he thought, after running a red light. No harm.

Fergal. Fergal Maguire. He'd had the two of them, Lara and the snake, crated up in the back of his van. Said it was stage equipment. Mad bastard.

The night was beginning to unblur. Where were they before the club? PJ Gallagher's. Doing coke off them rancid toilet cisterns. That's right, until Mark had decided to do lines straight off the tables and they'd been kicked out after some aul one had made a complaint.

PJ himself had done the honours, had even apologised. 'What can I do, lads,' he'd said. 'It's only nine o'clock and some people still want their quiet few.'

He'd produced a bag of blue pills, said he'd confiscated

them off a group of young fellas the weekend just gone. Threw them Mark's way; a peace offering.

Mark guessed that's where it had gone wrong – the pills popped, two each and three leftover in Mark's back pocket for later. The subsequent rounds of Jägerbombs in Magee's. Did they…yes, they'd been kicked out of there as well. Paulie Matthews, who was known as 'Lemon' amongst the lads after he asked for a wedge of lemon to go with a shot of tequila one night like a girl, had mooned a bouncer on the dance floor. Big hairy arse on him.

Mark indicated right, pulled into his parking space near the construction site. He was about to heave himself up when he remembered a bottle of painkillers Carmel had stashed in the glove box. He popped four in his mouth and swallowed them down dry.

At the site Mark looked around him. Most of the lads were there already, and they were all at least looking busy. Rory chatting his usual shite to the young fellas Dermo and Kev, sloshing his tea about in the one mug, the one mug Mark had told them not to use. The big white one that said THE BOSS in blue letters. The two Pádraics getting the concrete mixer going. The heads on them, no doubt they were out last night too. Vinny McGovern, playing a game of chicken with himself and his retractable tape measure. Dope.

What a sight for sore heads. Only a few months prior, this had all been a useless patch of fields, a blight of waist-high grass and feral nettles, nests of empty beer cans and torn up tents and fag butts, soon to be an entire estate of new houses. Two storey semi-Ds, paved driveways, 60 square metre gardens out the back. And if this estate was to go as well as the last one, they'd be finished up in the next six weeks and on to the next.

'Well, boss,' Clarky came limping over, docking an imaginary cap.

'Well,' said Mark, expelling a semi-solid lump from the back of his throat onto the gravel below as he began to walk in the direction Clarky had just come from.

'The priest,' said Clarky, falling into step with Mark, 'he's here.'

'Here? Where's here?'

'The office, boss.'

'Never trust a man who arrives on time, Clarky boy.' The cacophony of power drills and the hollering that inevitably starts up any time the angle grinder is turned on brought the pounding in Mark's head back into focus. 'Here, you don't have any of that, you know, from last night on you?'

Clarky gave a curt nod and in one slick flick of the wrist, placed a small bag of white powder into Mark's right palm. Mark thumbed through his keys, decided on one that had opened the front door to the first house him and Carmel had ever lived in together, back in the mid-90s when he was still working as a bricky for Les Callaghan. He dug out a bump of powder, sniffed hard, swallowed. Dipped a little finger into the bag and ran the powder over his gums.

'Right, where is he?'

'The office, boss,' said Clarky, pocketing the rest of the bag.

At the prefab that had been set up as an office space, Mark sat opposite the priest, both on soft-backed chairs with aluminium armrests, on the same side of a table littered with used mugs, papers, a closed laptop. On the other side of the room stood a coffee machine that spat out scaly Americanos at the touch of a button, an old Tupperware box containing individually wrapped custard creams and chocolate bourbons, a half empty pack of plain digestives, long gone soft.

On the walls was a calendar with a shining Ferrari Superamerica for November and some slips of paper with scrawled writing tacked up, an effort to remind Mark to file them away. Lopsided Venetians adorned the one window behind the desk.

Father Hyland looked a little lopsided himself. Worn and ragged about the edges. Hair, grey and thinning on top, could have done with a trim around the ears. Patchy face of a man who takes a drink. His jaw was set like someone who can hold their own. Although, there was something in the slight slouch of his shoulders and the way he fidgeted with his right hand – thumb nail tracing the length of his pinkie, then ring then middle fingers, back again – that gave him away as a contemplative sort.

The steely hooded eyes bored into Mark, reigniting his symptoms somewhat. He'd always disliked priests.

'Thank you for meeting me today, Mr Casey.'

'You've news for me, Father?'

'I do,' said Father Hyland, bottom lip protruding. 'The house, Monksfield. There's been another bid.'

'Oh?' Mark leaned forward. Business talk had begun. 'How much?'

The priest took a piece of card from his breast pocket, handed it over. Mark unfolded it, chewed his cheek for a moment.

'Who?'

'An American.'

Mark nodded, sat back in his chair. 'So?'

'So?'

'So, why are you here, Father?'

'The house, Mr Casey. Monksfield. I have some say, at least, as to its fate. And I'd like to have some idea as to whom it's going to.'

'Not about the money, then? That's a good one.'

'Not quite. The need to, you know, liquidate some assets is what's driving this whole thing.'

'We could all be a bit more liquid, Father.' Mark fished out a box of John Player Blues from his jeans, offered the box to the priest.

Father Hyland raised his palm. Took out his own box of Marlboros from the same breast pocket. The sound of lighters igniting. Grey smoke swirled in the air between the two. The priest crossed his legs, sucked his teeth.

'Go on, Father,' said Mark, antsy.

'I don't want to sell to just about anyone – if I can help it. There's a…matter that needs attending to and I fear a faceless pile of cash wouldn't be so…understanding.'

'Thought you said it was a Yank?'

'An American investor, yes.'

Mark dropped the stub of his cigarette into an empty can of Club Lemon on the desk. It gave a satisfactory sizzle as it hit the inch of liquid at the bottom.

'What's the matter, Father?'

'A…friend of mine needs to lay low for a while. And the house, well. It's the only place I can offer.'

'So, what? You want to sell me a house with a squatter included?'

'Mr Casey. I'm willing to agree to sell you the house for your last offer, if you agree to hold off on construction for six months. No more. I know you have plans to…demolish. Rebuild.'

'Duplexes.'

Father Hyland sighed deeply, face unaltered. 'Yes, Duplexes. You're expanding your operations out west and you already know that the selling price is more than fair. A profitable enterprise for you, no?'

'And what if this pal of yours won't budge in six months? What then, I just bulldoze over him?'

'That won't be necessary, Mr Casey. My friend doesn't want to hang around. Six months. Max.'

Mark considered the priest. Was there something pleading in his eyes? He was right, it was a good deal. But Mark enjoyed the pregnant pauses, the sight of a man squirming, even if he attempted to hide the fact.

Mark got up and made his way over to the coffee machine, made himself an espresso. He turned back to face the priest, swirling the hot liquid around.

'Knock off ten K.'

'Five.'

'Seven.'

'Mr Casey?'

'Yes, Father?'

'They're not that good a friend.'

A pause. Mark didn't like this shift. He swallowed the contents of his mug down in one regrettable gulp. Disguising the scalding his throat had just taken, he said with a nod, 'Fine. We've a deal. Demolition begins in six months.'

The priest took Mark's outstretched hand. 'Pleasure,' he said. 'Now, if I may make a quick phone call?'

'Course, Father. Help yourself to an old bicky and all.'

Mark emerged from the office, triumphant. He gave Vinny Mac, who had dipped away from erecting gutters at house numbers 13 and 15 in order to smoke a sneaky cigarette and play a game of snake on his phone, a mighty smack on the back.

'Jaysis, boss,' said Vinny, dropping his fag. 'My heart.'

'Where's Clarky? Go get Clarky,' Mark barked, shadowboxing the air in front of him. Vinny put the phone in his back pocket and turned, scanning the surrounds for signs of Clarky.

'Oh and Mackers?'

'Yes, boss?'

'You owe the lads a round,' said Mark, taking a cigarette from his own pack and wobbling it in front of the other man's face.

'How'd you know about that?'

'Nothing gets past me. What's this, the sixth time you've given them up?'

'One of these days—'

'Not gonna happen, Mackers. Ah, and here he is, the man himself.'

Clarky, making his way up the makeshift path to the prefabs with a half-eaten Double Decker bar in hand, gave a nod to Vinny and raised his eyebrows at Mark. 'Well?'

'Well – it's a done fucking deal Clarky, boy. Onwards and westwards we go.'

'Nice one, boss. What –'

The men all turned as the priest exited the office and walked by them, giving them a downward smile and glancing wave. A clumsy chorus of 'See you now, Father' and 'Cheers, Father' followed the priest through the metal railings and out of the building site.

'What say you,' continued Clarky, 'to a celebratory tipple?'

'I was in bad need of a cure.'

'PJs?'

Mark looked at his watch. 'Yeah, fuck it. There shouldn't be too many squares in there at this hour.' He turned to Vinny. 'Mackers?'

'Yes, boss?'

'Back to work.'

The two men walked off in peals of laughter.

Three pints of Coors, interspersed with slightly subtler bumps of coke, and Mark was feeling more like himself again.

'Same again, Clarky?'

'Absolutely.'

On his way to the bar, Mark made a detour to the Jacks. As he buttoned himself up at the urinal, he realised he was wearing the same jeans as last night. His hand went straight to the back pocket and, sure enough, emerged with three blue pills.

Things are looking up, he thought. As he headed back to the table, a brunette in tight grey trousers and a white tank top passed by, gave him a smile.

Mark rubbed his hands together with a suck of his teeth. Things are certainly looking up. He returned to Clarky with two pints of Coors and four shots of Jäger, placed the tray on the table and slapped two of the pills down next to it.

'Get that into you, boyo.'

'Unreal, boss,' said a smiling Clarky. 'Here, will the missus not mind you coming home laced again tonight?'

'Wife's away, the men can play! Her and the kid are staying at her sister's for the night. Off shopping or something.'

Now that he thought of it, wasn't Emma staying with that friend tonight? Isn't that what she'd said on her way out? *Tonight, I'm staying at hers.*

111

'Lucky fucker.'

'Mind your Ps and Qs, you,' Mark hiccoughed. 'And it's her that's the lucky one, can't get enough of me, she can't.'

Clarky laughed. 'Whatever you say, boss.'

'She can't. Sure, even this morning, she was sat on my lap, wet as a fish, caressing my face, whispering sweet nothings into my ear. Barely made it to work on time.'

⬤⬤

Sat on Mark's lap that morning, Carmel, after wiping a fleck of egg from the corner of his mouth, had been looking at her husband's eyes.

Brown. Definitely brown. Not even hazel. Brown as coffee. Or burnt toast. Or mud.

Mark closed the door behind him, prompting Toby to let out his signature gut-wrenching scream.

'Please, darling. You'll give Mammy a headache.' Carmel opened the cupboard next to the fridge, rummaged around.

Toby flung his bowl of Cheerios across the room. They were dry, at least.

Carmel opened the second drawer. Took out a packet of Solpadine and popped out three of the red pills, washed them down with a last mouthful of tea.

'Now,' she went over to Toby, writhing on the sofa. She changed the channel and handed him a controller. 'You play with that, and Mammy is just going to tidy up. Will you be a good boy?'

Toby was already glue-eyed, tongue out, mashing and tapping the vast array of buttons.

She drummed her fingers on the countertop, looking vacantly in front of her for some time. With a determined sigh, she turned and tied an apron around her waist. Took the dishes from the kitchen table, placed them in the sink, let the hot water run and gather foam as she wiped the crumbs and crusts from the table, letting them pepper the floor. Yellow Marigolds on, singing softly under her breath, *when the sun shines, we'll shine together, told you I'll be here forever*, as she scrubbed plates, forks, knives, frying pan. Wiped down counters, top of the hob, went back over the kitchen table. She got the sweeping brush out, started gathering piles of debris from the hardwood floors in deliberate motions, catching as many rogue Cheerios as she could find by the TV.

Upstairs, Carmel stretched the crow's-feet beside her eyes with thumb and fore finger. Yes, brown as they've ever been. Like Ferrero Rochers, she'd been told. Once.

Teeth brushed, face washed, creams applied. Yellow blouse, to brighten the day, put on and frowned at. It didn't look quite right with the black leggings but a cry from Toby decided for her: it'll do.

Downstairs, she scooped Toby up. Her back was immediately bombarded with tiny fists and ears rang with desperate 'no, no, nos' as she made her way to the front door, taking her Louis Vuitton from around the bannister in a practiced motion.

She bundled Toby into the car, took a red Nintendo DS from the back of the passenger seat.

'There you are, love.'

Toby flung the DS to the floor, Carmel leant across to pick it up, placed it on the seat next to him.

At her sister's, Carmel sat on the sofa finishing a cup of tea.

'Does Mark know you're going to dance classes?'

'Are you mad!' Carmel laughed. 'He'd think I'd lost my marbles or something. Maybe I have.'

'I think it's great, Car.'

'Ah. Are you sure now you'll you be OK with Toby? He's been in a bit of a wobbler this morning.'

'Don't worry, I love having him.'

'You're so good.'

'Come here, how's Emma doing? Haven't spoke to her since the party last week.'

'Ah, she's grand. Straight As, don't know where she gets the brains from.'

'From her auntie, obviously.'

'Obviously!'

'God, fourteen. Wouldn't you love to be that age again?'

'Ah stop. With all the spots and cramps and raggy nails?' Carmel, up now, putting on her coat. 'Right, I better head. Thanks again, Sibh.'

'Listen, Car,' Siobhan, tentative, lightly touched Carmel's left arm as she was about to step out the door.

'What is it?'

'I found him.'

'Found who?'

'You know,' Siobhan tilted her head to the side and lowered her voice to an almost whisper, 'Martin.'

Carmel blanched. She jerked her arm away from her sister and took a step back.

'Excuse me?'

'Come on, Car.'

'If you're implying something, come right out and say it, Siobhan.'

'No. I'm not. I just came across him on MySpace and thought…I don't know. That you'd like to know, that's all.'

'Well, I don't.'

'I'm sorry, I shouldn't have…I should have waited till you were back. I just…I want you to be happy.'

'I am happy.'

Siobhan bit her bottom lip, tried to reach a hand out to Carmel, pulled back.

'I know. I'm sorry. You're going to be late.'

Carmel looked hard at her sister, jaw clenched. She turned her head to Toby, who was examining a blue Lego block with a look of consternation. She sighed.

'We'll talk later, OK?'

'OK.'

'With wine?'

Siobhan smiled. 'I've a couple bottles in the fridge already!'

In the car, Carmel's fingers drummed the steering wheel, her lips sucked in. It had been Siobhan that had pointed it out to her, only a few weeks ago, about the eye colour. 'Toby's eyes,' she'd said. 'Never grew out of being blue, did they?'

The space between them had been filled with all that went unsaid. She'd known, then, that Siobhan knew something. But had no idea she knew about Marty. She couldn't remember mentioning him to her except in passing. This guy Mark works with. Funny. Carmel had called him funny.

She never called Mark funny.

The clock on the dashboard read quarter to one. She started the engine and drove off, head ringing with scraps of half-remembered conversations.

Carmel slammed down on her brakes. A young lad in a dark grey bomber jacket, greasy black hair and scooped shoulders, had crossed in front of the car. Zebra crossing. Shit.

'Dope,' the lad slammed his fists on her bonnet before walking off, middle finger held up behind him.

Hands shaking, she grabbed her handbag and popped the lid of a prescription bottle open, ignoring the car horn behind her as she placed two tablets in her mouth and swallowed before driving off.

The car park was almost full. Late. She was late. A minute to one. A space appeared and she pulled into it. No time to let the knot in her stomach form. She checked her hair in the sun visor mirror, reapplied her lipstick, grabbed her bag. In through the double doors of the community centre and quick steps past reception, down the corridor on the right, to a windowed door with a piece of paper Sellotaped to it: *BEGINNER SALSA 1pm.*

Through the window Carmel could see a group of people reflected in the mirrored far wall. Twelve, maybe fifteen. Mostly women, two men in their fifties. Kitted out in black and with their plimsolls and they all looked relaxed and as if they belonged there. Carmel's hand froze at the door. Instead of pushing, she turned to leave but collided with a woman, sixties maybe, short and stout, in black leggings and loose red tee shirt.

'Sorry, sorry!' The two women blurted in unison.

'Don't worry, pet. Here for the class?'

Carmel paused, unsure.

'Come on, we're late! Carlos'll be waiting.'

With that, Carmel was propelled through the door and into the bright white of the room beyond.

Heads turned and nodded. A few people waved at the older woman.

'Lily, come in, come in,' a tall slim man, thirties maybe, beckoned them in. 'And…?'

'Carmel,' she heard her name come out of her mouth before she'd realised she'd been spoken to.

'Just on time,' Carlos said, Spanish accent giving a playful inflection to his words. 'Welcome, welcome. Nice to see some fresh faces.' He smiled a big white smile in Carmel's direction, and from the nervous coughs and shuffles to her left she realised she wasn't the only one who was new there.

Carlos went to a CD player in the corner. Drums and trombone and steady beat filled the space. Half the class were already moving their necks side to side, smiles appearing and spreading down the line of them.

'We warm up,' said Carlos, taking his place in front of them, moving his hips in circles and jerks, arms bent and fingers clicking to the beat. 'Move your bodies, any which way. It's good to move, see, it's good to feel it, feel the rhythm. What salsa is all about: rhythm. Good, Gina, get the rest going, Lily, fresh as a chicken, keep going. Thomas, looking sharp. Come on everybody, you're here to dance. So, dance!'

Carmel moved her head forward and back a bit, tried to incorporate one of her hands to point to the beat. The two other newcomers beside her were much the same, until the lady called Gina, heavyset and in her forties, stepped closer to the middle of the room and wiggled her hips, navel-level breasts swinging with them.

The song ended and another started. A beat like someone tapping a cowbell counted time and the class instinctually moved their bodies in beat with it. Some their hips, some their shoulders. For Carmel it was her feet, tap tapping as she looked around her. Smiles complimented looks of half-bemusement, half-carefree joy. One of the men had his eyes closed, hands in loose fists as his torso jived along.

Carlos got the class to line up again as he demonstrated

some moves. Stand straight, arms loose but in control, step step this way, step step that way.

'Now you copy. Give yourselves some space. Watch me, and watch yourself in the mirror. OK let's go.'

He went through the same routine, slower, step step this way, step step that way. Carmel watched, stepped right instead of left, bumped into the person next to her.

'Rhythm will come,' said Carlos, 'for now, get used to moving. Good, good. Again.'

Six, seven, eight times they went through the moves, bodies learning to turn this way with arm out like so, or step from side to side with hips in constant motion. In the mirror, Carmel saw herself as clumsy and out of sync. She looked down the line and so was everybody else. A break in song, pause, grab some water.

'Carmel, yes? Carmel in the heels already, a pro. You're with me. The rest of you, partner up. No,' he pointed at one of the newcomers, 'you with her, and you,' he pointed at the other newcomer, 'with him, OK. Everyone happy, yes? Lovely even numbers. Last week I was dancing on my own, which is no fun. OK, make a circle, if you are two women then decide who is leading, OK.' He stepped to CD player and pressed play. 'Watch me and Carmel, we take it slow.'

Carlos turned back to Carmel, his hands reaching out to her, palms facing inwards.

'Take my hands, keep the space between us, we dancing together not on top of each other, yes. Stand tall, Carmel, that's it, nice tall backs everyone. Open position, this is open position, and now we dance. Ready?'

Step step back, step step forward. Step step right, step step left.

Carmel flushed as she tried to remember the moves, listen

to Carlos' instructions, watch the rest of the class, while trying not to catch herself in the mirror. There were fumbles, missteps, apologetic laughs. After a couple of revolutions of the circle it started to feel more natural. Carmel's steps fell in line with Carlos', she began to trust that he would guide her into the right spot, trust that she'd be able to follow the gentle prompts of his hands holding hers. Just the posture, the flair, the rhythm, feeling the rhythm in her body, was all she needed to focus on.

Carlos stepped away, changed the music. When he returned he placed his right hand on Carmel's left shoulder blade.

'Leaders, like this. You want your partner to feel secure. You feel secure Carmel?'

His did a tiny step backwards, bringing Carmel with him. Did a tiny step forwards and she stepped back into his palm.

'Yes,' she said, shyly. 'Very secure.'

'And your arm, look everybody, your left arm, Carmel, goes on top of mine. Relax it, relax it, don't push down, you are not trying to fight me, you want your body to be fluid, yes, like ink. Everyone, see like this, great, great. Now take my hand, good, and see our hands here are in the line with our elbows there. Closed. This is closed position. Everyone good?'

The class gave a chorus of uh-huhs and yeses.

'You don't sound so good but at least you all look good. We get that energy up. This music, you feel it in your hips, yes, let's go.'

Around and around they went, each pair in their own circle, the whole class in a bigger circle. Like planets spinning on their own axes, orbiting the sun.

Carmel watched Carlos in fleeting glances. Black hair slicked back, perpetual smile as he gave instructions and encouragement to the class. Thick eyebrows, not messy. A little chicken pox scar on his forehead.

Her hand on his shoulder blade felt warm. Strange, to be touching someone else. Another man. Even with Mark, his body had long lost its novelty. They made love, or rather, Mark would breath heavy on her neck in the dark of night and she would turn onto her back as he climbed on top, moved in and out of her for a few minutes and land with a grunt next to her. When had she last felt secure in his arms? When had she last been in his arms?

Marty.

She had felt safe in Marty's arms.

In Marty's arms.

Even the way he spoke made her feel safe. Real gentle, like. Rolled the 'ar' of her name, dragging it out slightly. A bit like Carlos, maybe. Almost like he was calling her 'caramel'. And he'd a tendency to soften words with a double 't', like he was lapping up milk. So he only had to ask her 'what's the matter, Carmel' and she'd be half melted.

He laughed too, after he spoke. Carmel never knew what was funny but something in the innocence of it, like he was trying to put those around him at ease, put her at ease, she was already at ease.

The first time. The excitement of her hands on new flesh, of new hands on her flesh. Desperate, almost. The longing that had built up between the two of them finally being acknowledged, indulged, set free, all at once.

The second time. The giddiness of the first time dulled. Pleasure soon giving way to an awkwardness Carmel couldn't place.

Then the third time. The time she had asked him over because Mark had snapped at her and had slammed the door on his way to the pub and she was alone and it was dark and raining out. When, afterwards, she had seen hurt in his pale blue eyes. A hurt deep within him, and now this, knowledge of a new hurt he was part of. She had wanted to bring him close to her and tell him nothing he was doing was wrong. That he was a salve. But he had dressed in a hurry and left into the night. Quit working for Mark the next day. Packed up, left. Not seen again.

Until her sister looked him up on the internet.

'You OK Carmel?'

Carlos shook her back to the room. Her body still moving, the circle still rotating.

'Yeah. Yes. I'm fine.'

'Transported to your own world, yes?'

'Sorry.'

'No need for sorry. This is the beauty of dance. You could be anywhere. OK class,'

Carlos stepped away, letting go of Carmel's hands. 'How are we feeling? Let's warm down a little.'

Carmel went up to Carlos after the class had finished their stretches and begun shuffling back out the door.

'How you enjoy that, Carmel?'

'Great, Carlos, really great. I just, I have to pay.'

'You're a natural, Carmel. A real natural. And yes, twenty-five for today.'

She took her purse out of her bag, 'I was so nervous at the start, but really,' she frowned, rummaging through the purse. Only a ten euro note in there.

'Yes, everyone is nervous at the beginning. Only natural, really. But dancing is the great equaliser, yes, the great unifier. Everything OK?'

'Yes, no. I seem to have left the cash at home.'

'Ah.'

Carmel, flustered, opened her bag and rifled through olds receipts and bottles of perfume, a hairbrush, some dusty M&Ms. 'I don't seem…'

'Well,' Carlos' tone gone flat. 'You are here next week, yes?'

'No. Well yes, I'll be here next week, but I only live around the corner. I'll come back, with the cash.'

'Well. If it's not too much trouble.'

'No, of course not. I'll—'

'I'm here til two thirty.' Carlos looked behind Carmel. 'Lily! Let me help you with that bag.' He stepped around her, leaving Carmel to watch herself redden in the centre of the hall.

She was sure she'd put aside the cash, had checked the night before that she had enough in her purse. It must have fallen out. In any case, there were some notes on the dresser.

What a fool, Carmel thought, and made her way to the car.

◗◖

'I took money from ma's purse,' Emma said behind her as she and Becca left that morning.

Becca had arranged for the two of them to buy a bag of weed off two lads from the boy's school. They had made the plans the night before, agreeing to go on the mitch. 'No one will notice,' Becca had said.

They had spent that night in hysterics, up until all hours as Becca told Emma stories of all the lads she'd shifted since the midterm.

'Not Frankie O'Brien?'

'Yeah!'

'With all the spots?'

'Yeah!' Becca had laughed. 'He kisses like a washing machine!'

Emma was yet to have her first kiss, while Becca had had ten, maybe even fifteen. Emma was still in training bras, while Becca had been measured in M&S, by 'some old one with cold hands and a creepy lisp,' and was already up to a C cup. Emma's frame was small and bony, while Becca had curves and walked like her hips were a pendulum, moving her forward with a grown-up fluidity.

Becca was confident and could stand up for herself. While that night, Emma hid from her phone and from the text messages she knew would be there, from the other girls in her class. *Lanky boy bitch – rich know-it-all bitch – kill yourself – frigid bitch – boo you bore.*

So, when Becca had floated the idea of bunking school, Emma hadn't taken much convincing. She would have followed Becca to Mount Vesuvius if it meant she didn't have to face the sneering and giggling from the corners of almost every classroom.

'They said to meet them by the back gates,' Becca had been talking the whole way to the park, not seeming to care if they were seen by other students or teachers. Becca paused, took off her school jumper, stuffed it in her bag. She put on a zip-up hoodie over the tank top she wore underneath, leaving it open just under her bust. She pulled the hoodie tight around her waist and fastened it with the bobbin taken out of her chestnut hair.

As they walked through the park, Emma noticed Becca walking a little straighter, head a little higher, shoulders back a little further. She was silent for the first time since they left the house as she scanned the park.

'Em,' she said.

'Yes?'

'Just…don't be afraid to say something, OK? These lads are cool, yeah?'

Emma felt her face redden. She cleared her throat, as if preparing herself for imminent conversation, wracking her brain for something interesting about herself that she might be able to bring up.

'There they are,' Becca exclaimed, quickening her pace. The ball in Emma's stomach tightened up again.

'Well,' said one of the lads in a dark grey bomber jacket and lighter grey tracksuit pants.

'Hi, Eric,' Becca said, like it was the easiest thing in the world.

'Who's your friend?'

Becca and Eric turned to look at Emma.

'Hi,' she managed, throat raspy.

'That's Em,' and Emma thought she saw Becca roll her eyes as she turned back. 'And you are?'

'Robin,' said the other lad, in light grey bomber jacket and dark grey tracksuit pants. He put out his hand as if to shake Becca's, Eric slapped it back down.

'So, twenty-five, yeah?'

Becca took out Emma's crisp twenty from her coat pocket and fished out her own euro and two euros from her trouser pocket.

'What's that?' asked Eric.

'Twenty-five euros,' said Becca.

'I usually only take cash.'

'This is cash.'

Eric laughed. Emma let out a slow outbreath, diffusing the tension that had built up inside her. He handed Becca over a small bag, half full of green flakes.

Becca took it, paused, pursed her lips. 'You wouldn't… roll one for us?'

The two boys looked at each other with a half grin.

'For you, Becca,' said Robin. 'Let's go over there.'

They headed towards a large sycamore tree at the edge of the park. Robin put his jacket on the ground, littered with helicopter seeds, and Eric reluctantly did the same. The four sat down, took turns in smoking the joint. It went round the circle twice and Emma felt a warmth rising up her neck and into her ears. She was painfully aware of how little she'd said in the past fifteen minutes.

'That's really good shit.'

'Don't tell me you're feeling that?' Eric laughed right at her, elbowing Robin beside him.

Robin laughed alongside his friend. 'Yeah, I didn't make it too strong.'

'She didn't even inhale properly.'

Emma turned to Becca, who didn't look back but instead joined in the laughter.

Emma's eyes prickled with tears. Her face grew hot. If only a chasm would open up in front of her so she could jump in and be swallowed whole. The urge to leave overwhelmed her. She got up, stopped herself from flat out running away.

'She's crying! She's crying!' Eric bellowed. Emma continued walking, wiping her face with the sleeve of her jumper, angry at herself for being so boring, for letting Becca down.

The park was quiet, on that mid-morning Thursday. Emma passed an elderly man on a bench, looking straight ahead of him as if there was a television set stuck to one of the trees. Two middle aged women strolled by, engaged in conversation. No one else was around.

She got to the other side of the park, to the little playground with primary coloured climbing frames for young kids. She hoisted herself up into the bright turret punched with squares and triangles on top of the slide. She sat sobbing, banging her forehead gently against the knees she hugged.

'Hey.' A male voice startled her. Emma looked up, saw Robin's head at the entrance to the turret. 'Mind if I?' He was already making his way up the three small ladder rungs. Emma slid herself into the corner, watched as Robin managed to fold himself into the rest of the space.

'You OK?'

Emma nodded, went to say 'yes' but her throat had closed up.

'I felt bad, you know. I wanted to check on you,' Robin paused. 'Not that I was following you, I just saw you come this way and…thought I'd come over. You know. To say sorry.'

'Where's Becca?'

Robin scratched the underside of his chin, faint baby hairs lined the jaw line. 'Her and Eric went off.'

Emma chewed her cheek, looking at her knees.

'She's funny.'

'Becca?'

'Yeah.'

'Yeah.'

Emma sighed. Picked at a hang nail on her thumb.

'There was actually a fair bit in it, you know. The joint.'

'Yeah?'

'Yeah.'

'Did you feel anything?'

'Sure,' said Robin. 'A little.'

In the moment's silence that followed, Emma took Robin in. Tall, too tall for such a tiny space but he didn't seem to notice. Mop of fair hair. Thick eyebrows. Picking absentmindedly at a spot on his cheek. He was relaxed, and that made Emma want to relax. She felt the tension in her shoulders ease up slightly.

'You smoke?' He said, digging out a slightly crumpled cigarette from his jacket pocket.

'Yeah,' Emma said, a knee-jerk response. 'Well, not really. They're kind of gross.'

Robin regarded the cigarette he had just lit, blowing out the smoke in a slow thin stream. 'You're right,' he said, and threw it out a star shaped hole to his right. 'My ma smokes, but I've always hated the smell.'

A fledgling laugh escaped from Emma's mouth. 'Me too.'

Robin smiled at her.

'You live in that big house near the sports field?'

'Yeah.'

'What's it like?'

She thought for a moment. It was the place she'd always lived. It wasn't like anything.

'It's nice. It's just a house.'

'It's not really though. It's like, four houses in one. Compared to mine anyway. Do you've your own room?'

'Yeah. Well, it's just me and my brother, so.'

'Oh. I share with my brother. It's chronic, he's a pig.'

'Do you've any sisters?'

'Yeah. Three. They all share the other room. Even more chronic.'

'I've always wanted a sister.'

'It's over-rated, trust me!' laughed Robin. 'Do you not get on with your brother?'

'He's only four. Spends all day playing bloody Halo.'

'On the Xbox?'

'Yeah.'

'A three-sixty?'

'Yeah.'

'Class.'

A young woman, dark skinned and stout, came into the park, pushing a buggy and holding the hand of a wide-mouthed, freckle-faced infant. He pointed excitedly to the slide, took his hand from his child-minder's, made teetering steps towards it.

'Come on,' said Robin. 'Let's go.'

'Where?'

'We'll just walk.'

Robin swung himself underneath the bar above the slide and in one jerky motion landed on the rubber floor below. He made his way round to where Emma was hoisting herself down at the top of the ladder steps.

'Your arm!'

Upright, Emma pulled her sleeve back down, hiding the criss-cross of scars.

'It's nothing,' she said, walking away from Robin towards the park gate.

'My sister does that too, you know,' he offered. 'Maybe it's a girl thing?'

'Yeah, maybe.'

'My ma thinks Veronica does it for attention, though.'

Emma kept walking, eyes to the ground. She tucked a strand of hair that came loose behind her ear.

'I don't know. I don't really like attention to be honest,' she said after a time.

They walked on in a somewhat companionable silence toward the town and up main street, each one following the other in no particular direction.

'Whatever people say about you, don't mind them. You're alright, you know.'

'Thanks.' Emma looked up at Robin. Wanted to ask, 'What do people say about me,' but he had put an arm out.

'Here, wait there.'

They had come to a laneway, tucked away in the back of the town. Emma had never really been down there, had only driven through it once by mistake when her mother had taken a wrong turn on the way to the swimming pool. Down it, Emma remembered, was a Polish shop and a newsagents her mother had said was run by Muslims.

Robin had bounded down the lane, leaving her standing on the corner before she'd realised he was off. Places like that always frightened her; dark, dirty, forgotten about. But if Robin thought it was safe, maybe it was. Maybe, she thought, I could just walk on through…to the other side.

She was just about to take a step forward when Robin emerged from one of the shop fronts, looking pleased.

'People always say I look older than I am,' he rubbed the back of his hand along his jaw absently. 'I got us something, come with me.'

Emma followed, at a much quicker pace than before. Robin was joyous, laughing and saying 'this is gonna be good' every few hundred yards. Emma couldn't help but laugh with him, although she didn't know what exactly was 'gonna be good.'

They reached a path that led down the canal, kept going to a secluded spot Robin knew about. They sat on a grassy verge, both on Robin's jacket, and he took out a ziplocked bag containing two white pills. They looked like the ones her mother took each evening for boosting her collagen.

'Now these,' said Robin, 'will get you high.'

Emma's eyes widened. 'Drugs?'

Robin laughed. 'Sure. Only – legal.'

He shook the pills into his hand, went to put one in his mouth and offered the other one out. He must have seen the uncertainty in Emma's face because he reiterated, 'I got them in that shop, Emma. They can't sell things to the general public unless they're legal, you know.'

Emma drew her lips in over her teeth.

'Sure, you were buying weed off me this morning. That's worse.'

'That's true,' ventured Emma. She couldn't exactly fault his logic.

'Ready?' he said, popping the lid off a bottle of Lucozade Sport. Emma nodded, let Robin place a pill in her mouth, like Communion, and swallowed it down with the bottle Robin had just taken a swish from. The ball of nerves tightened.

'Don't worry,' Robin seemed to read her mind again. 'The guy in there told me that this is, as you say, really good shit.'

They sat. Watching the featureless water, plucking up blades of grass. For a long time nothing happened. Impatient, Robin clicked his tongue on the top of his palate. He went to stand up with a decided 'fuck this,' but immediately sat back down again.

'On second thoughts –'

'Your eyes,' Emma marvelled. His pupils had grown the size of saucers, big black empty circles.

'*Your* eyes,' Robin shot back in equal wonder.

And Emma felt a swell of pure happiness. A laugh, more genuine than any she'd expressed in a long time, came tumbling out of her. Robin joined, the two a cacophony of joy. Her sides hurt, she hugged her belly, wiped her eyes. Head suddenly heavy, she lay down on the grass, feet toward the canal, white sheet of sky up ahead. A faint petrichor smell filled her nostrils. Turning her head to the side, a purple pansy looked back up at her, a tiny velveteen lion. A woodlouse furrowed amongst finger-nail sized twigs, making himself a new home. Nettles, covered in glistening silver prickles, sang songs of healing that mixed with the sounds of children's faraway laughter, forming a soft static blanket around her.

A ladybug, the deepest shade of orange and in perfect polka-dot symmetry, landed on her right hand, weighing her down for a whole blissful eternity.

Minutes, hours, days passed. Until Emma was awakened on earth with the sound of Robin, violently retching next to her.

Like a switch, Emma became painfully aware of a ringing in her ears, claggy mouth. She sat up. Itchy arms, itchy chest; itchy torso, itchy legs. Her entire insides wanted out, out of this skin it was trapped in.

'No,' Robin gasped, standing up and clutching his stomach. 'Fuck this, for real.' And he started walking, unsteadily, like that kid in the park, away from her.

'Where are you going?'

'Home.'

A wave of panic washed over her. She watched as he made his way back down the canal, not looking back, stopping from time to time to heave into the bottom of the concrete wall.

Emma found herself alone, body impossibly heavy. On the other side of the canal, a woman in bicycle shorts walked a spaniel, it tugging on the lead with front legs almost off the ground entirely. Somewhere, a magpie cackled. An insect buzzed and bored into Emma's head like a chainsaw. She was viciously uncomfortable. Couldn't find a way to sit that didn't feel like she was crushing her bones.

He's right, she thought. Fuck this. She got up, waited for the tidal wave in her stomach that standing had caused to subside. Headed in the direction of home. Her mother was away, after all, with her auntie Siobhan. Her dad was at work. She'd be able to lie down, in her bed, her lovely bed, without anyone knowing she'd mitched school.

She reached the front door, dropped her keys as she tried to unlock it. Her mother's car pulled to the kerb at the bottom of the driveway. Shit, thought Emma, I'm caught. She hurried with the keys, managed the lock the second time. She was about to run up the stairs, when she heard strange noises coming from the living room.

Grunting. Like someone in pain.

'Dad?' she stammered, opening the door.

In the middle of the room, her father. Jeans around his ankles, bare buttocks facing Emma.

Mark Casey spun round in a horrified heartbeat. 'Em –'

Carmel opening the front door behind. 'Emma? What are you –'

Someone on their knees before Mark. A female. Long brown hair and flushed face, wiping the side of her mouth, looking wide-eyed up at Emma and Carmel.

'Becca?'

6: 2018

ANONYMOUS

October 3rd, 2018, 5:46am

Nuala looked practically demonic tonight.

A sardonic laugh crawled from her lips when she caught herself in the grimy mirror of the prefab toilets. One of her eyes was hidden by a missing chunk of glass, the other trailed mist from an empty socket like a chunk of dry ice was lodged somewhere in her skull. Her hi-vis was skewed to one side like a luminescent cape.

Out in the hallway, the waves had reached the front door, rumbling across sand and plastic debris. With each flow, it carried more of the waste with it, retracting like the cringing arm of a beast testing the reach of its claws, before returning to lash the rubbish forward vengefully. It howled, that water, sang with the timbre of an abyssal wolf – incensed and mournful. A chorus of voices rose with it, a half-remembered hymn of ancient hatred.

When Nuala looked back to the mirror, she felt sick. Her phone was lying half-submerged in murky water, and the call time was running backwards. She opened her mouth to say goodbye, and a glob of black something flopped out. It was like passing a gall stone, she thought.

ANONYMOUS – 00:00:03, 00:00:02, 00:00:001.

Nuala raised her head, treacle-like spit webbing her to the page momentarily before she jerked upright. Black-brown vomit coated her keyboard and the files she'd been looking over, sticky like tar and smoky as ash. It wasn't the first time.
'Ah, fuck me.'
The monitor said 05:46am. She jumped a foot in the air as she shoved back the swivel chair, dashing into the toilet before she could get sick again. The wind rattled at the window frames and swept in under the front door of the prefab office, digging at folders and carrying a briny smell that stung the nostrils. By the time she reached the cubicle, her stomach had settled down, but she stripped the roll of blue towels and caught herself in the mirror on the way back to the office.
Nuala never had been called pretty – even her mother wouldn't lie to her about that. Born for wrinkles, Grandpa had called her. Deep-set eyes of a pale blue that always made her look manic or ill, lips you couldn't find to kiss under a microscope, and thin yellow hair. Not blonde, yellow. Like dirty straw. She also hadn't breathed properly when she was a child, Mam said, so her chin was non-existent, making it so her face sloped inwards at a sharp angle and her top row of teeth poked out. No, never pretty.
There was a knock on the door, rattling the frame. The lads were here. Given the time, they might have been waiting outside for her since 5:30.

'Fuck me,' Nuala grumbled again.

She gathered the blue towels into a ball and tried to sweep them across the files, leaving dark, grainy streaks on the paper. It would all need reprinting. The keyboard was ruined too, but that was a job for another time.

'Well? Are you up?' It was Nige, not Ruadhri. That was something, at least.

'Give us a sec!'

The mound of tissue in her hand was sodden and leaking, so she tossed it into the toilets and shut the flimsy cubicle. Stacking the files into a drawer, she went to the front door and threw it open. Nige stood in the wind and the drizzle, frowning under a thick woollen hat with the collar of his raincoat over his mouth. Nige had a great chin, and it was like he drew his black stubble on every morning with a fine-edged pen.

'What the fuck? I've been down there with ages.'

'Sorry, I know, sorry. I was on the phone.'

'Who does be calling you at this hour?'

Nuala pulled her hi-vis from the rack beside the door and slammed it shut behind her, locking up. 'Ah … I've a brother in Vancouver. Calls me sometimes, when I'm on late.'

Even in this light, she could see his suspicion before indifference took over. 'Right. Give me a hand with this so, yeah?'

Nuala unhooked the keys from her belt and tried to act casual, swinging them around her finger. Two and a half years she'd been doing this – ever since Brexit, or thereabouts – and not once had there been a living soul down by the water at this time. Yet still she got nervous, every time she and Nige (or Ruadhri) made the long march down the dry dock to the loading area. A glance from a curious jogger, a nosy neighbour with designs for local council, a fisherman headed down to the boathouses early, that's all it would take. News travelled fast here. By lunch, everyone in town would know something wasn't quite right. And wasn't that exciting? More exciting than anything that had ever happened to Nuala, that was certain.

'Did you see the match?' she asked Nige. He watched hurling and porn, so far as Nuala could tell, and somehow, she doubted they were close enough to discuss the latter.

'Which one?'

He never asked that before. 'The … the one on TG4.'

'I flicked through it a few times. I've to watch that shite on mute. Can't be listening to those auld lads spitting all over their microphones. I haven't a word of it.'

'Same,' Nuala sighed. 'I should've gotten one of those exemptions they have now.'

'Wouldn't that be fucking nice.'

It took Nuala a few minutes to unlock the gates – for how much the council invested in security, you'd think they would have more than a chain link fence to stop people getting down to the storehouse.

'You ever hear of Kurt James?' she asked Nige as she held the gate open for him.

'Mental case,' he muttered, and led the way onward.

Nuala scoffed. '… Yeah.'

Nuala liked Nige a little less for that – she listened to Kurt James all the time. He was a pastor from the US, a podcast host and a country singer. Very wise altogether. He said most world governments were plotting to depopulate Earth. Nuala wondered if the Dáil was in on it. Hard to imagine. If there were TDs at these top-secrets meetings of the New World Order, Nuala could only ever picture them fetching the coffee for shadowy figures sat around smoking cigars. She chuckled to herself.

A pair of headlights appeared down by the water, and the same white Transit that always came along appeared on the incline to the storehouse. One thick, fleshy arm of hairy muscle dangled out of the driver's window, snatched at the wrist by a gold watch to match the gaudy ring on the pinkie finger. Nuala never saw who drove the van. She didn't particularly want to put a face to Sherley's reputation. She usually just stood off to the side and let the lads do their work.

The storehouse itself wasn't used for much these days – a few lorries came by to load up on toiletries and wholesale foods for the supermarket in town, but little else. Back in the Celtic Tiger, they expected this place to be a budget Galway Bay, thronged with trawlers and carriers that needed careful management and thorough administration to keep straight. Nuala supposed that's where her job had come from, but nobody ever came around to question whether she was really needed. She was part security guard, part secretary, part longshorewoman. Her payslips came from a faceless public sector payroll address. Minimum wage, but that suited her just fine. She didn't have anyone to take care of.

Nuala opened up the storehouse for two sullen young men who bundled out of the van without so much as a nod. Nige wandered over to Sherley's window with his hands in his pockets, and they muttered to each other as the young fellas moved their cargo out. Nuala rarely got to see what it was they took – crates and suitcases, most of the time – but she could picture it. Fireworks. Cocaine. Maybe even guns, but she doubted it.

Then Nige was standing in front of her again, blowing on his hands. 'Sherley wants me to take you up to Monksfield.'

'Why?'

Nige's eyebrows shot up at the question, like he'd never met someone more brazen in his life. 'Because he wants me to. Hop into the car.'

Nige started off down the slope towards the water, and Nuala risked a glance back as she followed. All she could see of Sherley was his arm, tapping gently on the van door as the lads loaded up their packages. She could make out a pair of eyes glinting in the low light like beads of dark marble. Pig's eyes, she thought. He certainly looked the kind of man to eat you, if your corpse fell into his pen.

Nige's car was hardly anything special, but he made her kick the dirt off her boots before she sat in. He drove in silence, occasionally looking out over the water at the streetlights rippling along its surface as they blinked on. It was only then Nuala began to think what Sherley and the lads might be doing while she was gone. She chewed her lip trying to think of what might be on her browser history. Nuala didn't have much to do in the office most nights, so she sometimes got … curious.

'He won't be checking my computer, will he?' she blurted.

'What?'

'Sherley. I don't want him going through my stuff.'

Nige looked at her out of the corner of his eye. 'Listen … There's some shit Sherley might have to move through the storehouse over the next few days. He doesn't want you anywhere near it until it's safe.'

Nuala shrugged. 'I never go near –'

Nige tutted, bumping a little in his seat as he lurched over a pothole. 'This stuff is sensitive. We won't be doing it the normal way. It needs to stay overnight in Monksfield, and he wants us watching it.'

Nuala tasted the vomit from earlier all over again. 'But what about the storehouse? I'm on the night shift all week …'

'Forget about that. Sherley will make sure you're taken care of, and then some. Besides, who'll come looking for you?'

Monksfield House was a spectre, floating over town in a world of its own. Nige's car struggled up the once-elaborate driveway, the windows scraped by briars and low hanging branches as they ascended. Older than sin, it was, the only of its kind still standing on this street – the rest had been bulldozed by contractors a decade ago to make room for some kind of Americanised super-mall. Nuala wondered whether An Bord Pleanála used the blueprint to literally wipe their arses.

It was a heritage site now. Protected from destruction, yet in no fit state for human habitation. Nuala might have laughed at the irony, if the sight of the husk didn't remind her of a wheezing old man, crouched in his forgotten corner waiting to finally collapse with horrible relief. Grandpa had been like that, towards the end. Barely able to breathe, yellowed eyes bulging as he took a drag.

Nige had the key, somehow. Nuala never really gave it any thought – Nige and Ruadhri seemed the type of lads to be able to get their hands on anything, if it was wanted. The door jammed every few inches as he shouldered it inwards, leaving a semi-circle of chalky white on the floor inside. They switched on their phone torches to guide their step, dust motes falling like snow from the creaking rafters.

'We've to clear out a space upstairs,' Nige mumbled, taking the steps two at a time and disappearing into one of the bedrooms above.

Nuala loitered in the foyer for a moment. Ten years' worth of grey dust blanketed every surface, disturbed only by their footprints and the odd border where a photograph once hung from the wall. Nuala followed Nige up as far as the doorway of a large bedroom, and saw him standing amongst a heap of discarded memories – crates similar to those that sometimes came to the warehouse, broken furniture left as nothing more than mangled kindling, dolls with manic eyes and toy cars that hadn't seen a driver in decades. A stack of papers was propped against the far wall, and Nuala gravitated toward it, peeling back the spiderwebs. A pencil sketch of a model aeroplane was on top, bound to the others in frayed string. The shading, the scale, the detail – it wasn't bad.

'This fucking place …' Nuala shook her head. 'Who knows what them poor people went through. All them battered women, and the young lads who had nowhere else. Where do you think they ended up?'

Nige stiffened over a box of Christmas decorations, then ran a hand through his hair frustratedly. 'Are you going to help or not?'

By the time they were finished, an effigy of withered lives decorated the foyer, launched down the stairs without too much care to land in a pile, kicking up waves of dust and making the floorboards shudder. Nige left Nuala coughing in the aftermath and came back from the car with an inflatable mattress, a sweat-stained pillow and a blanket that wouldn't have been fit for a dog. Maybe it was dogs they were moving here, now that she thought of it. Sherley seemed the type to go fishing around for a microchip with nothing but a Stanley knife and two of his meaty fingers.

'There must be good money in the dog trading over there, yeah?' she asked.

'I wouldn't know. Listen, me and Ruadhri will pick you up from your place, tomorrow night. Make sure you've slept well. If you get caught dozing off, I'm not standing up for you.'

Nuala scoffed. She was the most excited she'd been in years. The most awake. The most alive. But a panic bubbled in her chest suddenly. She was in it, now. No plausible deniability. No claims of being taken advantage of, when the Guards came a-knocking with torches and search warrants. She eyed the mattress. A few dogs, that was all it was. Surely, that was all.

Her home wasn't a place to be proud of, she knew that. A sliver of kitchen running alongside a musty sitting room, the corners stacked with old beer cans, every ashtray caked with black dust. The couch was streaked and stained; pillows frayed to the point of almost falling apart at the seams. She saw that. She saw it all. But even the notion of cleaning, of getting anywhere near a pair of rubber gloves, gave her a sickly feeling and made her want a cigarette. Then she'd spend a few minutes on the couch, smoking, rationalising that she would never have the time to do the whole job at once, and therefore it couldn't be done.

'And to all the listeners out there,' Kurt James said, his voice muffled from where her phone rested against an empty pizza box on the coffee table. 'Prepare. Watch, listen, and prepare. Something is coming. Something that will humble the unready, and vindicate the wary. So you ask yourself – which one do I want to be? The sceptic who waved away every warning of societal meltdown, threw out the word "prepper" like an ignorant curse? Or the silent bear, hungering no more, content and safe in your hibernation through that initial surge, that initial crash? Only to wake, and rise, and live. Let's pray, listeners. Let's pray.'

Nuala turned down the volume and settled back into the couch, watching the dawn creep across the once-cream carpet towards her feet. She'd get on that, soon. The prepping. She hadn't met anyone half as into Kurt James as she was – not this side of the Shannon – but there were pages and websites and communities. Many times, she had written posts in the dead of night, hoping to catch the Americans awake, only to delete them unposted.

'ANY1 ELSE FEELIN LYK THEIR LOOSING THEIR MIND'
'HELP – LOOKIN FOR PARTNER, FEMALE, PREPPER FELLOW LISNER'
'VRY LONELY, DON'T THINK ANY1 REMEMBERS IM HERE'

She was staring into space again, her eyes burning and half-shut with the strain of the morning light that had now spread across her torso and splashed warmly across her face. Her alarm went off. 08:00.

When she opened the front door, there was a man standing in the porch, hand upraised to knock. She winced even as she almost barrelled into him. This was far from his first time knocking. It was just the first time she'd answered.

Vampire rules applied, where Tarran Hyland was concerned – she was meticulous in never inviting him past the threshold. It was a vampiric kind of name. Like a comic book villain, or an oil baron from a Spaghetti Western. She could imagine him as a Victorian detective with a name like that, complete with pipe and Sherlock Holmes hat.

But instead, he was a priest. She'd never met a young priest, and Tarran Hyland was grey and dry as one would expect, but there was a youth in his step. An ageless strength in the way he took her in with sage eyes. It was an almost convincing get-up, for someone who represented what he did.

'Nuala, good morning,' he said, hands clasping quickly behind his back. Like a principal, about to discuss her newest detention. Nuala had gotten detention a lot.

'I'm in a rush, so if you could –'

'Oh, of course,' the priest stepped back, hands upraised in apology. He followed her as far as the door of her car. 'But I did promise to check in on you.'

Nuala froze with the keys in her hand, glancing at his reflection in the window. He loomed past her shoulder, warped by the glass into a misshapen shadow. She turned, gripping the keys until they dug into her palm.

'So, what, you have the God-given right to come harassing me? What did Grandpa tell you, that I'm disturbed? He loved that word, so he did.'

'Harassing? Nuala, I …' The priest swallowed, taken aback. 'He never said … that word. It was his last wish, to know that someone was … Maybe I made a mistake.'

'Maybe you did. I don't need your help.'

She left him in a scattering of gravel.

Oakville Heights was a few minutes outside of town, kept private by a stand of trees that encircled the front garden and made it all but invisible from the road until you were up on top of it. The driveway was a tight strip of brownish gravel flanked by manicured plots of imported grass, slotted together like a jigsaw and trimmed neatly to the verges every morning. Nuala rolled down her window, listening to the inviting crackle of the gravel under her wheels and catching a long whiff of the freshness of the place. It made her feel soiled in comparison sometimes, as though when she touched that doorbell she would leave behind a slick of oil.

But when her finger fell away from it today, as any day, it was clean. She caught herself in the polished reflection of a window, and tutted. She had stuck her head under the shower and changed into a blue chequered shirt with jeans, trying to look somewhat fresh, but the illusion was thin. Her eyes were crater-like, to the point she could barely hold her own gaze, and when she checked her teeth, they were just as yellowed as they'd been before brushing.

Nuala was just about to buzz again when Kayla emerged. A plastic tray was balanced on her arm as she bowed gracefully out of the door, empty dishes stacked neatly on top – she had a way with the old ones, especially the men. She could get them to eat every last bite, like nobody else. She slowly twirled with the dishes, never in danger of dropping them, every movement an artful dance … Olive skin gleaming in the soft morning light, her raven black hair left to hang down to her waist, straight enough to slice through you and shining like an obsidian mirror. When she saw them, her smile burned through Nuala, reaching every part of her slender face.

'Well, would you look,' Kayla grinned at Nuala. 'We can't keep you away, can we?'

'No,' Nuala replied faintly. 'No, I suppose you can't.'

'Come on through,' Kayla went on, drifting into the common room at the end of the hallway ahead. 'Marg was saying she might put you on cleaning with me, today.'

It wasn't news to Nuala. She'd asked for it. Begged for it, even. If she could help it, she'd spend the rest of her life picking up wet towels and dirty underwear with Kayla. She'd never known someone so vibrant, never spoken to someone who made life feel so fiery and dynamic. When Kayla laughed, the existential sludge fell away from Nuala in clumps, like she was being pulled from the world's grey jelly to set her feet upon real ground for the first time. Her first day at the nursing home, they had sat on the lawn and shared a Lucozade. Kayla said she could never finish one by herself, too sugary. When Nuala asked if she had a glass to pour the rest into, Kayla had grinned, 'Just use the bottle, sure. I'm not poisonous, I promise.'

She was, though. Kayla was poison, to Nuala. Not like a snake bite or a death cap. More like a cigarette. Or a lethal injection at the end of a hard, unforgiving life of constant failure.

The common room was bright and garishly painted, as if the yellow and pink motifs would somehow offset the withered-follicle grey and blood-clot red of the residents. The breakfast tables were being wiped down and prepared for board games and puzzles, while the social carers led a steady stream of walking frames, wheelchairs and canes out the big PVC back doors into the private gardens behind the building. Nuala quickly counted the heads. Twelve. Two less than when she was last here.

'Morning!' Marg vibrated over to them in her small, bouncing gait. She was a woman of strange proportions – large, round head and bust, thick shoulders that wouldn't have been amiss on a rugby pitch, but legs that looked entirely too small to support the rest. She didn't brush her teeth very well, so they were just as stained as Nuala's, yet she smiled often and unashamedly.

Nuala grumbled through the pleasantries, standing close enough to Kayla that she could smell her perfume. Nuala suddenly realised she hadn't put on deodorant. Did she stink? Would Kayla ever mention something like that, even if she did? Nuala glanced over her shoulder. The priest was loitering near the hallway. Their eyes met again. She felt nauseous.

'Right, let's get to it, so!' Marg all but yelled, clapping her hands to speed over to the priest. The two of them ducked into one of the occupied rooms and were gone.

Nuala was dead on her feet after the long night, but Kayla kept her going. Random bits of news, little jokes, smiles thrown in Nuala's direction when the conversation stalled and they folded towels in silence. They brushed and mopped the corridors, stripped and made the beds, bleached the toilets, did the washing, emptied the dishwasher … things Nuala could never have done at home. Things that made her feel like tearing her skin off, anywhere else but here. Anywhere else but with Kayla at her side, pottering around like the world wasn't the way it was. Like it wouldn't end, someday soon.

'What do you know about the local priest?' Nuala asked hurriedly, sipping grainy coffee in the kitchenette. 'Not the main one. The old fella.'

'Who, Father Hyland?' Kayla bit into a digestive delicately, her pinkie raised like an aristocrat. 'He's some man. He was the one behind Monksfield, apparently. Used to live there, as a boy.'

Nuala glanced at the door instinctively and raised the cup to hide her grimace. He knew. He knew something, and now he knew her face. That nosy fucker, why couldn't he have left it be?

'I heard all sorts of horror stories from there,' Nuala muttered.

Kayla snorted dismissively. 'All that about packing babies off to America? Jesus, Nuala, don't be telling me you're some kind of conspiracy nut, now.'

'It happened in other places.'

'Exactly,' Kayla shook her head. 'But not here. Why do you be asking about Father Hyland? He's a good man – you know, Marg even told me they tried to hang him out to dry. The Church, like. Some big inquiry into his funds, years ago. But he's the real deal, God bless him. He's not some trafficker.'

Nuala's head spun around, words spilling from her mouth like blood from a fresh wound. 'Don't trust those fuckers, not a one of them. I'm not into all that … conspiracy theory stuff … but I've read articles. I've listened to podcasts, like, and … I could show them to you, if you wanted. It's all out there, if you know the right places to look. I could show you.'

'I'm alright, thanks.'

Kayla said those three words with the same grin she held from before, but the joy had left her eyes. Nuala saw something else there now – fear, or maybe suspicion. Nuala shrunk away from it, but she knew it was her own doing.

'We had better get back to it,' Kayla said, still keeping up the façade as she washed out her cup and slipped past Nuala into the corridor.

A few minutes alone, that's all it had taken, for her to wring the warmth and the hope and the benefit of the doubt from Kayla. Now the other woman was looking at her like everyone else did.

It made Nuala angry, exposed, vulnerable … Now, they were closer than ever.

If Nige was a wire brush, Ruadhri was a scourge.

He came for her that night, heralded by a single full stop sent in a text. She finished her cigarette and stamped out the butt amongst the other four she had all but swallowed in anticipation. Ruadhri's car was a classic black Lexus, but despite that he didn't seem as perturbed by her crusty boots as Nige had been. He barely acknowledged her when she sat in, hardly waiting for her to strap the seatbelt across her chest or close the door before he rolled out of the driveway. Ruadhri lived like a man who had borrowed all of his minutes from a particularly impatient devil … or maybe he just couldn't permit himself to dwell on one thing for too long. Then again, Nuala didn't figure him for a man of conscience.

'Where's Nige?' she asked. It was like Ruadhri pulsed silence himself, the way the air in the car felt heavy when all was quiet.

'He's there already. We had a few bumps earlier, he's cleaning up.'

Nuala swallowed the taste of burning in her throat. 'Shitting themselves, are they? The dogs?'

Ruadhri drew those words into himself like a vacuum, and they didn't bounce back in the form of a reply. His hands, already white-knuckled against the steering wheel, tightened further. Not meaty like Sherley's, those hands, nor slender like Kayla's – somewhere in between, the upper phalanges softened by ginger hair that matched the sparse coarseness around the back and sides of his bony head.

'Don't let me hear about you fucking sleeping again,' he said finally.

Nuala scooted a little further from him. 'Sorry.'

Ruadhri's car took the ascent to Monksfield gracefully, squeaking to a halt in the shadow of the manor that lay across the gardens. It no longer reminded Nuala of a dying man – sometime since last night, it had transformed into a beckoning stranger at the end of a black alley, whispering 'Come and see what I've got. Come and see.'

Ruadhri let them in with his key, and shut the door promptly behind Nuala, locking it again. The dust had settled again over the pile of debris she and Nige had left at the foot of the stairs, like the house was reclaiming its possessions, swallowing its treasures back into the monotone greyscale it had cultivated over the years left untouched. Nige came thundering down the stairs at such a pace, Nuala thought he might bust through one of the rickety steps. When her eyes adjusted, she spotted a red scratch on one side of his face.

'You fucking deal with her,' Nige breathed at Ruadhri. He hardly glanced at Nuala before undoing his belt and disappearing down a hallway to the broken toilet.

Nuala didn't dare to question Ruadhri as he gestured for her to follow him upstairs. Her eyes were stiff with the strain against the dimness, and her face had gone slack and numb with the exhaustion. She blinked rapidly to account for the deepening black they stepped into – and almost fell back down the stairs at what awaited.

There were no dogs. The pillow and blanket from the other night were thrown haphazardly into the corner, and sitting on the bare floorboards was a woman – a girl, to be truthful – cradling her own body with her arms crossed over her knees. Dyed blonde hair, orange vitiligo of splotchy fake tan in the dark. One of her feet was bobbing with adrenaline, and Nuala heard her sniff back tears as they stepped in.

'I leave for half an hour,' Ruadhri said. His voice had changed; it was matter of fact, almost gentle now. 'You told me you'd behave yourself, Jodie.'

The girl was perhaps seventeen, by Nuala's reckoning, but by her dark eyes she had seen enough of life in those short years to last a century, and little of it good. Jodie could have been a hundred, with eyes like those. She glanced at Nuala fleetingly before fixing her gaze on the floor in front of Ruadhri's feet.

'When is Sherley going to be here?' Jodie asked, her voice thick with the dregs of a recent breakdown. 'I want to talk to Sherley.'

'You'll see him soon enough,' Ruadhri replied, then stepped into Nuala's space and muttered, 'Go down there again and watch the front door. I'll take the first watch up here.'

A thousand questions flashed across Nuala's mind, but got stuck somewhere in her throat. She simply slipped away, and heard Ruadhri pull over a stool for himself. By the time she reached the foyer again, Nige had emerged, leaning up against the wall to rest his eyes. Nuala stalked over to him, with all the intention in the world of telling him no, that she couldn't be a part of this, whatever it was, that even with absolutely nothing riding on her life and freedom, she wouldn't take the risk.

Instead, she asked, 'Who is she?'

Nige rubbed the mark on his face and winced. 'Sherley's daughter-in-law. Or she would be, if she hadn't dodged the altar on the day of the wedding.'

An obscene, irrational envy washed over Nuala, and she drew a cigarette from her dwindling supply. A contract for companionship in her lap, and this Jodie had thrown it away. There was shame beneath the resentment Nuala felt for the girl's decision, but it came and went with the intake and exhale of her first drag. Kayla in a wedding dress, that would be a sight. Nuala could buy a suit and act like she ran things for a day, then give herself over body and soul to Kayla's every whim for the little time that was left for the world.

'So the husband wants her back?' Nuala asked, pulling another long drag.

Nige shrugged. 'She's going to Longford in a few days, that's all I know. The son is sending some lads over. Then it's their problem.'

'Doesn't sound like she'll be going back to the altar.'

He shrugged again, a master of the indifferent I-see-nothing front. 'I doubt it.'

In fact, he was so indifferent it offended her. Not on Jodie's behalf – that was its own thing, and Nuala still wasn't sure she could feel any pity for such an ungrateful girl. But for herself.

'You're not afraid I might tell someone? About her.'

Nige stood up straight and sneered. 'Not really. No.'

She blinked. Maybe he was right – what good would bringing the Guards down on herself do? And what would Sherley do to her, if this was how he treated his own family? She didn't once think about the money Nige had promised. That didn't matter. It was better to be a nobody with a secret than a nobody in a prison cell. Or a car at the bottom of a lake. Besides, what did she owe to the girl? What did she owe to anybody? The buzz came back – that feeling of existing beyond the sphere of what her life had become.

Before she could answer, Nige moved on, taking up a position on an abandoned couch in the adjoining room. 'I sleep first,' he mumbled. 'You swap with Ruadhri in a few hours.'

Nuala posted herself up in a room just as empty as any other, with skirting boards that may once have been white, now a sickly pale green with the various growths along its edges. Nuala didn't mind sitting on the floor as she pressed play on the latest of Kurt James' podcasts. She skipped the opening prayers and settled in, turning up the volume. It all melted away – Nige's snoring, Jodie starting to sob again, Ruadhri's warnings for her to stop, even the incessant creaking and crackling of the house itself. When she caught the slap of skin on skin upstairs, she turned the volume up some more.

'And we say up to the Lord ...'

She was in the prefab again, a roll of blue paper wrapped around one hand as she swept bubbling mess from the desk. It stained everything it touched, seeped into the grain of wood and fabric as she wiped uselessly.

'Give us a sign ... Ready the watchful and the attentive for the collapse that comes ...'

Brackish water spilled across Nuala's feet, a few inches soaking up the filth and carrying it back out the door. She glided across its surface, leaning out into the hallway. The front door was ajar, jammed up with broken toys, discarded furniture, paintings, rusted machine parts. She gripped the handle and jerked the door inwards, fighting against the escaping surge of the water.

'He's not a trafficker. Not like you.'

The words shattered across Nuala's face like a broken bottle, and suddenly her feet didn't glide anymore, they went with the flow, the door was gone, she was being sucked out into the swell. The taste of ash was in her mouth, ash and blood and salt, and staleness, staleness, like the fumes of something rotting inside her belly. She tried to halt herself, snatching for the passing rubbish, her fellow passengers ...

but they fell apart in her grasping hands, turning to mush, turning to moss, turning to dust.

The water stilled. Nuala was drifting in the doldrums on a sheet of black glass. Someone was muttering in the sky as she lay her head back on the steady rhythm of the current – Grandpa, or Kurt James, or maybe God. It was dark up there, too, clouds of bloody cotton before a nothingness so deep she had to close her eyes to keep from vomiting. When she opened them again, the girl from Monksfield was lying alongside her.

'I didn't mean to scare you,' Nuala said. It made sense to say it to this girl, even if she didn't look like Kayla.

'Who'll come looking for you?' Kayla asked sadly.

A man with headlights for eyes was standing over her.

Nuala stifled a gasp when she woke.

Nige still snored on the couch in the next room, and all was quiet upstairs. She checked the time – 22:05. An alert on the screen asking if she wanted to shuffle play some more of Kurt James' sermons. She crept onto her feet, stuck in a low crouch for a moment. Her heart felt unsteady, thudding behind her eyes like it was about to rupture.

'Fuck this,' she breathed, and slid through the dust and the grime to where Nige lay.

She knelt by him for an eternity, watching the uneven bumps in his pockets as though she could lift the contents out with her mind. He mumbled in his sleep, ever so lightly, one arm cast over his face and the other dangling over the end of the couch, so that he looked like one of those old romantic paintings. He looked normal, asleep. He didn't look like someone who did the things he did. Nuala envied him. He could go out into the street and act like a real person, with real feelings and real dreams. She just pretended to ignore what she knew people thought about her, what they said, the jokes they made, the mistrust, the disgust.

The opportunity arrived when Nige shifted further onto his side, exposing his right pocket where she could make out the shape of his keys. She held her wrist in her other hand to steady it, and with thumb and forefinger gently prised the pocket open with a soft inhale. She caught the ring itself and slowly, ever so slowly, pulled. The keys came loose easier than she could have hoped, and just as she was cradling them into her fist to keep them from jangling, she saw eyes peering out from under Nige's arm. Bleary, unrecognising in the first few seconds of half-dream. She froze, gripping the keys to her chest, waiting for the shout, for Ruadhri to thunder down the stairs and …

'Just a few more minutes, Father,' Nige grumbled, then rolled over onto his other side.

She didn't move for a moment, listening in disbelief to his low breathing. Then she was gone.

Nuala had known it was wrong, the first time she followed Kayla home from Oakville.

She didn't set out to do it that morning, nor did she even have it on her mind when they parted ways that afternoon. It was just … very easy to do. Kayla had invited her over for a cup of tea once – well, she had mentioned where she lived and suggested she and Marg might drop over sometime. So it wasn't like Nuala wasn't supposed to know where she lived. But something kept her from ever reaching the driveway. It was nicer to watch Kayla go about her day when she didn't know Nuala was there; it meant she had no inhibitions. It meant Kayla didn't feel she had to put on her earth-shattering smile or put on any friendly airs. Nuala could watch from that spot around the corner all day, trying to imagine what it would be like to take Kayla by surprise, just walk up behind and embrace her, and they'd joke and kiss and maybe share a Lucozade again. And then Nuala could keep her close, keep her safe.

That had been the plan, ever since the day she saw Kayla in the shop. Asked about her in the post office, on the pretence of a package wrongly delivered for Grandpa. And when he got sick, she'd gently suggested Oakville. And when he died, they were only delighted to have Nuala on as a volunteer, a thank you for all the comforts they'd given him in those last months.

Tonight, there was no time for watching. She had thought about where Kayla might have to stay, if things got tense, if she wanted to leave again, if maybe she didn't like Nuala after a while. She hadn't even begun preparing to have another person in the bunker. It wasn't a bunker really, more like a reinforced shed out near Benbulbin, but it would serve until things had settled. There would no leaving, not until Nuala was sure the coast was clear. And something about tonight … the collapse was coming. The end was nigh.

Nuala knocked six times in a short, jovial beat. It would put Kayla at ease, this late, especially with Nuala arriving in a car that wasn't hers. At least she thought it would – the frown Kayla wore on her smooth face when she opened the door a crack said otherwise.

'… Nuala?' she croaked, groggy from sleep. 'Is everything alright?'

'Of course you'd ask that,' Nuala grinned. 'That's so you. Always looking out for people. Yes, everything is alright for now. But I … I'm here to help you.'

Kayla didn't plaster her frown over with any jolliness this time. It continued to deepen like a sinkhole that Nuala was on the edge of falling into. She edged the door a little further open.

'What do you mean? Nuala, are you drunk?'

'Drunk?' Nuala scoffed. 'No, no … I'm … I'm trying to save your life.'

Kayla's head tilted in what Nuala hoped was affection. 'I don't need saving, Nuala. I'm alright, see? I'm fine.'

'You're not, though. Nobody is, because … Because something bad is about to happen, I read about … there's a solar flare, they said it was going to be a few years off, but they're lying. And then there's the Middle East, and everything there, and there's always going to be someone trying to profit off it. Did you know there's a chance we could be at the end of our cycle? The planet, like. Humans.'

Nuala clamped her mouth shut, and Kayla watched her. It wasn't affection. It was pity.

'I don't think I'll be in tomorrow.' Kayla began to shut the door. 'Go home, Nuala.'

Nuala lodged a boot into the narrowing crack and shoved her face into the gap. 'Wa – Wait. Wait, this is the only chance I have. I think they might kill me, when they figure me out. Look.' She jangled the keys where Kayla could see them. 'Look. See?'

The door loosened around Nuala's foot, and for a moment she dared to hope, as Kayla stepped out into the moonlight with her robe pulled close around her. 'Nuala, you're obviously in some distress, or maybe you're on something, I don't know … But if you don't get off my property, I'm going to call the Guards. I don't want to, but I will.'

'If you just come to the car –'

'Get the fuck off my property! Now!' The curse sounded all the starker, all the more real, coming out of a mouth as perfect as hers.

Nuala almost did something very bad, then. But headlights swerved on the road just as she began to move toward Kayla, washing the driveway in light momentarily. Nuala whirled. A car had come to a halt behind Nige's, at the foot of the hill. The door slammed and locked behind her, and Nuala didn't even grieve Kayla's vanishing. She ran.

There was a hedgerow bordering Kayla's garden to the east, inland. She made for it, boots squelching in the grass and sending up sprays of brown water. She heard an engine rev somewhere in the dark, and she burst through the hedge, briars tearing at her jacket. Her hi-vis jacket, she realised. She let the passing branches rip it from her shoulder and kept running. Soon, she was turned around, in a grid of half-matured fir trees planted in their neat rows, replicas of each other in every direction. She picked a path and ran some more, spitting out tar, sucking at the air like a beached fish.

When she broke the treeline again, the car was waiting on a dirt track ahead. Not a Lexus. An old Fiat, chugging smoke out the back. The man who stood in the beam of the headlights was not Nige, nor even Ruadhri.

The priest stepped out almost calmly, but with his first step he wobbled. 'I'm not supposed to be driving, you know.' An unsteady hand clasped the car door and he swayed until he was upright again. 'Old injuries in the legs. Father Greaney will be livid with me.'

Nuala gaped through blurry eyes. 'What the fuck are you doing out here?'

'Eh, I don't know … Keeping promises. Or maybe I'm just … wandering around.'

She gasped for air, edging around so he faced her in the light, and she could see him properly. He looked like a farmer out for a nighttime stroll, with his wellies and long coat, but for the pang of whiskey she caught down-wind of him. His jaw hung looser than before, his eyes unfocused and swollen.

'How long have you been following me?' Nuala asked, keeping her distance. 'You're not supposed to follow people. It's not polite.'

'No. No.'

'Fuck off, then. You're pissed, I can smell it.'

The priest leaned on the open door, forcing out a dry chuckle. 'Not nearly as much as I'd want to be. Greaney keeps a tight fist on the liquors, these days. I just want … to talk.'

Nuala squinted at him in disbelief. 'I don't know how you thought this would go, this Batman shit, but I'm not entertaining it. Get out of here, before I call the Guards. I'll have you taken away, you creepy fuck. I mean it.'

The priest's stare hardened. 'Ring them, go on. You might have some explaining of your own to do.'

It sounded ever so vaguely like a threat, even if he could barely stand. Nuala let her feet carry her backwards a few steps before turning on a heel and marching onward into the shadows.

'You've gotten yourself into something, haven't you?' he called hoarsely. 'Up at the old house?'

She whirled, all her previous anger flaring back up in a glut of stomach acid. 'That place is just for you, is it? All them poor women and children – you had your fun back in the day, I'd say!' Before she knew it, she was in his face, so she could almost taste his fiery breath. 'And now you're standing here like you aren't part of the biggest cult in the world, telling me –' She coughed, and stepped away, trying to catch her breath.

'You know, it's people like you, too busy begging Sky Daddy for your just deserts in the next life to do anything about the shit-show in this one! People like you got us to where we are.'

He watched her under heavy eyelids, unblinking. 'Maybe. But I tried my best.' He shut the door and edged his way around using his hands, until he sat back on the bonnet with a sigh. 'After this morning, I told myself tonight would be the last time. The last time I … checked in. Except when I walked up, you weren't alone.' He shrugged, but it was like there were weights laid across his shoulders. 'I don't really believe in intuition, or coincidence. I don't think I do.'

Nuala scoffed. 'What, God sent me a raving drunk, did he?'

He drifted for a moment, as though sweeping aside the spectral cobwebs of old memories. 'Your grandpa was worried, in the end. Wanted to know you'd be looked after, when he was gone.'

Nuala glanced behind him, but the night was dark and silent besides the two of them out on the trail. She crossed her arms, breath rattling phlegmy in her chest. 'Did he tell you I was disturbed? He loved that word.'

'It would run in the family, wouldn't it? Your uncle Larry and all?'

Nuala made to grab the front of his coat, maybe throw him in the dirt, take the car, whatever else she needed to do … But when she met the priest's gaze, she found something familiar in it. She'd seen that horrible clash of hope and despair in her own face, those nights when she dreamt of that filthy mirror. She slid down onto the bonnet beside him. She was tired, so *tired*.

'I'm not some dribbler in a strait jacket …' she said half-heartedly.

He only nodded.

'And all that at the house, I'm done with it. I want … nothing to do with it anymore. I just want … her. She's safe with me.' Nuala chewed the inside of her cheek until she tasted blood. 'She doesn't know how to do it on her own.'

'Do what?'

'Anything. She doesn't know what's coming, but I do. I can teach her how. I know I can. And in the end, she'll thank me.'

The priest's breath steamed in the headlights as he exhaled. 'I don't think so, Nuala.' There was a phone in his hand, she saw, and he placed it between them before he stood ungracefully.

'What are you – ?'

'I won't speak a word of this.'

He wandered along the beam of light away from the car and stood out there in the night, holding his coat tighter against the cold and humming some old tune. She glanced at the phone. It was unlisted, and three nines glowed at her expectantly.

Nuala clung to the wreckage of her world as it ended.

She pressed the button.

- FIN -

The Writers

The authors in this collection are members of a gathering of writers drawn from the graduate cohort of the MA in Creative Writing at the University of Limerick.

Seán Coffey lives in Galway. He has twice been shortlisted for the Francis MacManus Prize, also for the Hennessy Prize, and other competitions. His work appears in the Hennessy Book of Irish Fiction 2005–2015, The 2003 Phoenix Collection of Irish Short Stories and most recently in the literary publications, *SWERVE*, *The Ogham Stone* and *Crannóg*.

Máirín Stronge is a writer from Mayo, living in Westmeath. Her short fiction has been Long Listed by Fish, shortlisted by New Irish Writing, placed second in Dalkey Creates Festival, published in *The Ogham Stone 2022/2023* and *Washing Windows III*. She is writing a novel, a contemporary story of love, loss, redemption.

Sharon Guard is a writer from Dublin. Her work has appeared in New Irish Writing, SWERVE, *The Ogham Stone*

and the *Washing Windows* anthologies. She won the Molly Keane Creative Writing Award in 2020 and her story 'Artifice' was shortlisted for the RTÉ Short Story Competition in 2024. Her debut novel, *Assembling Ailish*, was published by Poolbeg Press in February 2025.

Gio is a writer based in Killarney, Co. Kerry. She enjoys exploring different forms of creativity. Her work has appeared in Listowel Writers' Week winners' anthology, *The Ogham Stone*, and *Washing Windows III*. Her work has also been broadcast on Dublin Digital Radio, West Limerick 102 FM and Radio Kerry.

Sarah Lou Ryan is a writer currently living in Kildare. She has read and loved books, words and writing stories from a very young age. Her work can be found in *Flash Fiction Magazine* and *Gypsophila Magazine*. She likes to explore humanity, experimenting with speculative fiction and magical realism.

Conor Clohessy is a writer from County Clare, who began his career in theatre, with his plays *Scum of the Heavens*, *The Ballad of Wesson's Boys* and *Tales from the End* performed at the Jonathan Swift Theatre in Limerick throughout 2018 and 2019. Conor has since completed his BA in Journalism, with plans to produce a fantasy novel soon. He is also studying at the Lir Academy in Dublin as part of their renowned BA in Acting.

Acknowledgements

One day in 2021, we stopped being strangers.

Not all at once, mind – the vehicle of our fateful meeting was the MA of Creative Writing at the University of Limerick, some of us part-time, some of us full-time. But over the course of our one or two years together, we were blessed in our exposure to the work of dozens of fantastic writers.

For many of us, never had there been an opportunity to surround ourselves in this creative culture before. It seems surreal, almost, to think we walked into a building every morning with the likes of Donal Ryan, Sarah Moore Fitzgerald and Joseph O'Connor, getting to pick their brains for all things writerly and coming away with lasting impressions of our own styles and ideas.

The foundation of our AdNibs Collective is an homage to the feeling those mentors cultivated – pure exultation in and respect for our imaginations, that we could share with each other, and eventually the rest of the world. A special mention must be included to Bob McDonald, who first put our collective's name to page and helping us with the first reference points from which to create the world you'll experience herein. We wish him all the best with his own creations!

Bringing this particular project to the publishing stage was a challenge none of us had faced before, with Helena Mulkerns providing some much-needed industry wisdom and Mary-Jane Holmes lending us her editing ear after our own diligent drafting over the course of the final few months.

Thank you, of course, to the friends and family who have withstood the sound of the keyboard clicking away, the grand pontification about whether to spell it Tarran or Tarren, and the endless loop of telling people in Zoom meetings that they are on mute. And a special thanks to you, the reader, for letting us tell our stories.

Máirín, Sean, Sharon, Gio, Sarah-Lou and Conor

451
Editions
www.451Editions.com